True Colours

True Colours

Rhian Tracey

BLOOMSBURY

First published in Great Britain in 2007 by Bloomsbury Publishing Plc
36 Soho Square, London, W1D 3QY

A CIP catalogue record of this book is available from the British Library

ISBN 978 0 7475 8941 9

All papers used by Bloomsbury Publishing are natural, recyclable products
made from wood grown in well-managed forests. The manufacturing processes
conform to the environmental regulations of the country of origin.

Typeset by Dorchester Typesetting Group Ltd
Printed in Great Britain by Clays Ltd, St Ives Plc

1 3 5 7 9 10 8 6 4 2

www.bloomsbury.com

For my lovely, patient parents Helen and Rob Tracey, who hung in there during the dark and turbulent teenage years.

'I love you all the colours.'

'Careful what you wish for,' always seemed such a stupid saying to Rosie. Why would you want to be careful about your wishes? Wishes were things that remained firmly in fairytales. Everyone knows that blowing out the candles on your cake and wishing can't guarantee you anything. Wishes should be spur of the moment things. But just imagine one of your wishes coming true. It would be like winning the lottery, having the perfect hair day every day and never, ever having a single spot again.

Any one of these would have been Rosie's perfect wish, but she never thought she would be granted her one. When she was, Rosie was caught off guard, which might account for the traffic lights thing . . .

☆ Rainbows ✳

It wasn't just strange that her mum had agreed to go to the fair; it was the fact that she was prepared to let Rosie wander around, on her own, for a whole hour. Ever since she was little Rosie had loved fairs. The promise and excitement they held always appealed to her. She loved the thrill of the big rides; the noise, the music, the mouth-watering smell of candyfloss and hot dogs, and above all the hope of adventure. Rosie often felt her life lacked any real sense of adventure. Rosie's mum seemed to have had something against fairs. If they had been at home, instead of on holiday, there would be no way that this would happen. If they were at home her mum would have kept her under a much tighter rein. She would mutter at her about strangers and kidnappers, as if Rosie were three instead of nearly thirteen.

Flora and Daisy were her two best friends. The three of them had a lot in common, difficult parents, a lack of real pocket money, the desire to be out and about on their own and, of course, their floral names.

But Rosie wasn't with Flora and Daisy. She was with her mum, staying at her grandparents' house by the sea. And tonight, for some unknown reason, without her grandpa even having to step in and back her up, her mum had sighed, gathered up her brown leather handbag and car keys and said in a reluctant voice, 'Come on, then. Let's go, if we're going.'

Rosie didn't hang around to ask why, she didn't even have time to apply lip-gloss or change her clothes. Appearances had to take a back seat. This was a one-off, a chance of a lifetime, and she was not going to miss it.

Rosie imagined she would have to spend the evening trying to persuade her mum to let her on the rickety sounding roller coaster or the dangerously fast looking Waltzers, so she was gob-smacked when her mum looked at her watch and gave her an hour to wander about, on her own. It just wasn't like her mum to trust Rosie to do anything like this. The 'dangers of strangers' had been drummed into Rosie from an early age. Her mum had always insisted on making sure she was never on her own, even though she was now a teenager – well, almost.

But Rosie wasn't stupid; she wasn't going to argue

10

with her mum about this new sense of freedom. Maybe now would be a good time to ask about a raise in her allowance, but before she had a chance her mum had gone. Rosie was free!

Rosie wasn't sure where to start first. Everything looked so fantastic, bright and enticing. She didn't even care that she was on her own, as most rides were for large groups of people, like the Mexican Hat and the Waltzers. Rosie went on them all anyway. After buying some lurid looking neon pink candyfloss, she wandered around the stalls to see what they had to offer – that was when she came across it.

Florien's Fate and Fortunes did not look like much, and normally Rosie wouldn't have been attracted by it, but then this wasn't a normal evening by any means. If she'd been with her friends, they wouldn't have looked twice at the little green tent that looked like it belonged in a campsite. If she'd been with her mum, she would have dragged her off, muttering about rip-off merchants and time wasters. But tonight Rosie was alone and she could make her own decisions without being influenced by everyone else in her life.

She hesitated outside the tent. Five pounds was very expensive for a fortune-teller and it meant she wouldn't be able to go on anything else. Rosie looked at her watch. She only had ten minutes left before she had to meet her mum and she didn't want to be late. But her curiosity was too great – she chose to pay the money and enter into Florien's world of Fate and Fortunes.

Rosie wasn't sure what to expect as she sat down on what looked like a camping chair to wait for Florien. She had never met a fortune-teller before. She'd seen gypsies camping in fields by her gran's and she had watched the odd TV programme on clairvoyance and psychics, but she wasn't really sure of the differences between them all. Her stomach was turning over as she waited for someone, presumably Florien, to come out and reveal the secrets of the future.

When Florien finally appeared from behind a curtain, Rosie saw that she was a fairly normal looking person dressed in jeans and a T-shirt. She looked like someone's mum except for the jewellery. She wore more jewellery than anyone Rosie had ever seen before but, strangely, it looked all right on her.

Florien sat down and stared intensely at Rosie for what felt like a long time before she spoke. Rosie began to feel a little nervous and out of her depth. She wished she had Daisy or Flora with her, so she could giggle away the odd feeling she had in her tummy. It was too late to jump up and run out now. She didn't want to look like a little kid.

Florien began to speak to her in a quiet but calm voice. She spoke without any of the drama Rosie had been expecting, without the crystal ball and the melodramatics.

'Welcome to Florien's Fates and Fortunes. Florien cannot be with us today but I am Brianna and I am here instead. You are very curious. You want to know everything about everyone before your time. You wish you could predict the future. You wish you knew what was around the corner. You wish you could see into people's minds. Yes?'

Well, that was a lucky guess. Anyone coming to see a fortune-teller would wish all of those things, surely? Rosie was beginning to feel that perhaps her mum was right. Maybe it was all a rip-off. Maybe these fortune-tellers were all con artists. As Brianna continued, Rosie wondered who Florien was and why he or she wasn't here telling her fortune. She felt a little let down by the replacement.

'You are not alone in this but you are different. You have unanswered questions. Things you know you cannot ask. There are things you cannot bring up.

These secrets affect you but no one will talk of them. No one will mention them and this bothers you. You hate secrets. You feel everyone knows something you don't. You live in the dark, in a house of secrets and the unspoken. And all you have is the picture.'

Rosie gasped, then quickly tried to look relaxed – but she couldn't. Brianna had just summed up her world. She had told her exactly what her life was like. But how did she know about the picture? No one knew about the picture. Not Daisy or Flora, not even her mum – especially not her mum.

Rosie was now completely hooked. She was going nowhere and she would have paid anything to this woman to hear more. She knew this was her only chance to get answers to all her questions. Questions which had been building up since she was old enough to eavesdrop. Since she was old enough to notice that things weren't quite right at home. There was a lot that she didn't know and even more that her mum deliberately kept from her, including the picture.

'The picture is your secret. It's the only one you have. It is safe. No one knows of its presence. It is the picture which will eventually reveal all to you. It is the picture which will open your eyes and let you see, telling its own story. But you are not ready for that yet. In the meantime what I can do for you is to let you see a little better, no longer just in black and white, all right? I can help you see in colour and this will reveal a little more to you. I will help you to build up your jigsaw and fill in the missing pieces, to complete the picture.'

Then she stood up, smiled and left the room. Rosie was once again on her own and very much in the dark.

Rosie sat in the camping chair for longer than necessary. She was aware that she was getting pins and needles in her feet, which she hated. She felt she was outstaying her welcome but she needed more. Rosie needed the fortune-teller to explain all this seeing in black and white business. What did she mean, she would help her to see in colour? She already saw perfectly well and in colour. She didn't even need glasses. So what was she on about? She hadn't told her the future or her fortune. She had just mumbled on about jigsaws and other rubbish. But then she knew about the picture – Uh oh! Rosie glanced at her watch and saw that she was at least ten minutes late. The fortune-telling session hadn't felt long. If she ran all the way and appeared out of breath her mum might not ground her for life. It might get rid of her pins and needles, too.

On the way home, in the car, Rosie thought about what the fortune-teller had said. She barely spoke to her mum until she noticed that her mum looked pretty preoccupied, too. She clearly wasn't in the mood for chatting. Rosie realised she didn't even know what her mum had done for the hour that they had been at the fair.

'What did you do while I was on the rides, then?' Rosie enquired as they came to a standstill at the traffic lights. Her mum was far too busy staring into space to reply. Rosie repeated her question, a little louder this time. She wasn't sure her mum had heard her above the noise of the radio. It didn't seem tuned in. All Rosie could hear was the fuzzy buzzing noise when the dial is between stations. She leant forward to turn the radio off but saw that it wasn't even on. Maybe she was getting a headache. She did feel funny. As if her stomach were still turning over and a bit dizzy. Maybe there was too much sugar in the candyfloss. Her mum absent-mindedly answered Rosie's question.

'Oh, I just wandered about, got a cup of horrible coffee off one of the stalls, dreadful greasy places. What about you? What rides did you go on?'

Rosie looked closely at her mum as she replied and couldn't help but notice how bright the traffic lights were down here by the seaside. They looked brand shiny new. It was as if they had lit up her mum's face and hair in a red glow, as if she had a halo around her but in the wrong colour.

Rosie told her mum about the Mexican Hat and the roller coaster and the candyfloss but decided to leave out the part about the fortune-teller. It didn't seem worth troubling her mum about it. She knew there would be an argument to follow if she did. As Rosie looked down she noticed that the traffic lights must still be on red as her own face and top were glowing brightly, too. For some reason her mum started pulling away, accelerating briskly into the road, into the traffic! Rosie screamed.

'Mum! What are you *doing*? Stop! The lights are still on *red*!'

But when she looked up at them they were green. Rosie looked at her mum and then at herself in the passenger mirror attached to the sun-visor. Both their faces and tops were glowing red as if the light had been shining on them. She could have sworn that the traffic lights were still on red. She must have been wrong. She must be ill. The pins and needles were still lingering in her feet, and perhaps she had sun-stroke, too.

Rosie's mum shook her head and carried on driving, laughing at Rosie's hysterical outburst. The laughter finally broke the tension that neither of them wished to acknowledge. Rosie tried to put the incident out of her mind. She felt really silly for shouting and overreacting but she thought they were going to cause an accident. Her eyes must be playing tricks on her. Flora had glasses and looked very cool and sophisticated. Rosie wondered whether she should get her eyes tested before she went back to school.

They were going home tomorrow and Rosie was secretly glad to be leaving, even though she knew her mum wasn't. It was lovely seeing Gran and Grandpa but she missed her own room and her friends and maybe even school. It would be good to get back to normal and then maybe her mum would ease up a bit. She had been really tense and moody lately, and Rosie was getting fed up with it.

Rosie said goodnight to her grandparents and went up to bed. She had always been put in the attic room, even when she was a baby, but now it felt too small for her. It had roses on the wall and roses on the bedcovers and even roses in a vase on the windowsill. Although Rosie knew her gran had decorated it for her in honour of her name, it was a bit much now she was a teenager. Well, nearly a teenager. Even the boats and shells in the bathroom had begun to annoy her and feel a bit too seasidey.

Nothing felt real here, as if life was on hold and the real world was carrying on around them but they were paused in 'holiday time'. She'd just had enough of coming to the same place year after year. She had tried asking her mum why they couldn't go somewhere different but there was never a clear answer. Her mum dodged the question, like so many others Rosie had tried asking before. Rosie knew she'd feel much better when she got home. Both she and her mum were a bit strange at the seaside cottage. She couldn't work out why. She normally put it down to the fair arriving, which would end in an argument about why it wasn't safe for Rosie to go. Not this time though.

When Rosie got into bed, she tried to write down everything the fortune-teller had told her, but her head was banging and her eyes were all fuzzy. She only managed a few sentences and key words. She couldn't work out how the fortune-teller could have known about her photo. 'The picture is your secret,' she had said. It was true. Rosie kept it hidden in a book, *Dr Star's Signs of the Times*, and looked at it pretty much every night, but she hadn't told anyone about it, not ever. It was too much of a secret and too much of the unknown. What would she say? That she had taken a photo from her mum's cupboard of some man and now kept it as a bookmark? It would sound odd, more than odd, strange and weird. But when Rosie looked at the picture and looked into the man's eyes and saw his crooked smile it was like she knew something else was in this photo, just not what – well, at least not yet.

'The picture will reveal all' was what the fortune-teller had said, but it hadn't revealed anything in all the years she'd had it. She'd often thought about throwing it out but just couldn't for some reason when it came to it. And now she was told it would help her, would tell her all the things she wanted to know, apparently! Rosie remained sceptical; perhaps her mum was right and it was best not to trust people at fairs.

She decided to call one of her friends instead to take her mind off everything.

'I'm even looking forward to school starting back. And we'll be in Year Eight at last!' Rosie whispered down her mobile phone, telling Flora how bored she had been and how glad she was to be coming home tomorrow.

'That's what weeks in the middle of nowhere do to

you,' Flora breezily replied, having spent most of the summer in some exotic villa somewhere. 'Makes you actually look forward to school. Ooohh, you don't think you might be coming down with something, a bug or the flu, do you, Rosie? I mean, wanting to get back to that dump! Mate, you must be bored. Anyway see ya laters, dude!'

Rosie hated feeling like this, ungrateful. If it wasn't for her grandparents they wouldn't have a holiday at all. Her mum would work through the summer and send Rosie to summer school. In comparison she supposed staying with the grandparents wasn't so bad. It was really pretty at the cottage and she loved the sea and the cliff-top walks. She always took Treacle with her for walks, when he was up to it. Treacle was her grandparents' old chocolate Labrador – at least he was company. It just felt like there was nothing to do there on her own.

One summer she'd brought Daisy and Flora with her and that had been much better. But they were both abroad this year with their families, who went on proper holidays.

Rosie enjoyed consuming vast quantities of 'garage food', as her mum called it, on the journey home. She looked forward to the stops at several service stations along the way, purchasing the highly overpriced magazines, sandwiches, family-size bags of crisps and cans of Coke. This was the best part of travelling: eating and talking and listening to the radio. Rosie and her mum took it in turns to listen to their preferred station. Rosie loved hearing her favourite DJ's smoky voice and husky laugh, especially when she talked about her kids. Rosie couldn't help wishing for a slightly more relaxed mum herself.

Her mum definitely had good points though. For example, she could drive all the way home without once looking at the map. This was impressive to Rosie, who could not map-read to save her life. Geography lessons were a testament to her failure in this area. Flora's mum had a posh Mercedes with a satellite navigation system in it. An American lady told you when to turn left and what road to get on and when to turn off the motorway. Flora said after a while her mum starts talking back to the woman. She then starts swearing at her. Eventually she turns the woman's voice off as she gets far too annoying and does things to Flora's mum's blood pressure.

Rosie couldn't really see the point in it but Flora's mum always had to have the latest gadgets. Rosie's mum was very old-fashioned by comparison and liked tradition with a capital 'T'. Hence the holidays in the UK when everyone else in the whole wide world was abroad in the sun, having holiday romances and getting a tan. Rosie always seemed to come back a little bit red with more freckles, but definitely without a tan. Apart from last year when she took a sachet of fake tan out of her mum's magazine, applied it in her gran's bathroom and ended up a violent orange colour which stained her new shorts. Not to be repeated.

Rosie flicked thorough her copy of the latest issue of *Heart* magazine and turned to her favourite section, 'Star Gazers'. She scanned down the columns until she came to her star sign. She read:

This month you must seize the day! Gather ye rosebuds while ye may – so, get in there, girl! Go for it and stir things up a little. Expect fireworks on the thirteenth and take that risk on the thirtieth. You know you should have taken this risk last year – go on, you won't regret it!

While Rosie's mum was muttering under her breath about exits and junctions, Rosie stole a quick look at her. She seemed to get more relaxed as they moved away from the seaside and back into the city.

She was looking a bit sunburnt this year, which was odd as it hadn't been that hot this summer. Her mum usually wore factor fifty so that she wouldn't burn and took every opportunity to slather Rosie in it, too. So why she was red Rosie didn't know. Maybe she was having a hot flush if she was that age. Rosie wasn't entirely confident about what hot flushes were about, but she'd heard her gran mention them a lot. Maybe her mum was suffering from road rage? Or had she overdone the blusher? Gran was always telling her she looked pale and should make more of herself, whatever that meant.

Rosie decided not to mention the redness of her mum's skin in light of endangering her improving mood. It was probably the prospect of having to go back to work. Working in a hospital seemed to suit Rosie's mum, who worked as a sister in the local A & E department. She took her job very seriously. In fact, she took life very seriously, unlike Rosie.

There was no way Rosie was going to be a nurse, or work in a hospital with all that stress. Rosie was going to work for a cool magazine, something like *Chick* or *Heart*. She was going to be an astrologer, too, no matter what the teachers said at school about getting a proper job. Astrology was a proper job; someone had to write the columns – people depended on knowing their stars. It was how most people made their important decisions. Rosie was the best at guessing people's star signs and working out their destiny. She consulted her bible, *Dr Star's Signs of the Times*, daily, much to the amusement and sometimes frustration of her mum. Maybe if Rosie's mum believed in her star sign, things would work out better for her. It couldn't hurt to try, thought Rosie, as they pulled into the parking space in front of their flat.

Red

There was something exciting and nervous all at the same time about the first day back at school in September. It was as if there were a million possibilities awaiting Rosie at the school gates. A new uniform, new shoes, bag and pencil case helped. It made her feel more grown up to be moving into Year Eight and wearing a different tie to Year Seven and knowing her way around this year. Rosie was determined not to let Flora or Daisy put a dampener on her good mood with their traditional moan on the school walk.

This year she wanted to enjoy herself and not get in trouble and not worry so much about everything. She wanted to have fun and more importantly she wanted to have fun with Toby McGregor. Not that she would ever tell anyone else this, not even Flora and Daisy, it would be too embarrassing.

'God, I can't believe the summer is over already and we're back here on our way into The Deepest Pit of

Hell!' moaned Flora somewhat predictably as she slammed shut her front door, shoving a stick of chewing gum into her mouth with careless practice. Rosie rolled her eyes. It was always the same with Flora. After every holiday or break they had, she made such a fuss about going back to school. As if there was any choice! Flora was one of those people who couldn't wait to rush through the next four years, get to Year Eleven and get on with her 'real life'.

As they walked to Daisy's house Rosie noticed that Flora didn't look as tanned as she usually did after four weeks in their family's villa in the south of France. In fact she looked a bit green as she complained half-heartedly about Miss Wilde, their form tutor, and Mrs Lennox, the Headmistress, and Mr Phinn, their Head of Year. She was ranting on about how there was nothing to look forward to in The Pit. Maybe the prospect of another four years of this really was making Flora feel ill. Rosie didn't have a chance to interrogate her, though, as once they picked Daisy up the three of them were in full flow, chewing, talking, laughing and comparing notes from their respective summer holidays.

'We had a wicked time in Tuscany; we did the whole touristy thing and then just relaxed by the pool

27

at the villa. It was excellent; everyone had such a cool time. Dad hired a people carrier from work and we travelled down in style. We even had DVD players in the back, how amazing is that? But yeah, the boys were a nightmare, annoying and ganging up on me the whole time. Really wound Mum up – but then that's not hard, is it?! Ha, ha, ha!'

As Daisy excitedly filled them in about Italy Rosie noticed that she seemed to be going quite red in the face whenever Flora asked her any questions about her family. The more questions Flora asked the more Daisy looked as if she were blushing, which was most unlike Daisy, 'Miss Cool, Calm and Collected'. She was also really loud, almost shouting, and was beginning to give Rosie a headache. Rosie wondered if Daisy was a bit embarrassed knowing Rosie had been stuck at her gran's again, for the millionth year running, and felt sorry for her. Who knew? Rosie was more than a little confused by the changes in her friends as they approached the school gates. They were trying to hide from Mr Phinn the Deputy Head, so they wouldn't get a late card. That really would give Flora something to whinge about.

When they got to registration Miss Wilde had already handed out everyone's new timetables and other letters home about various different matters. All of which Rosie's mum would read studiously that evening.

She was on the PTA and very involved in school life. This was not such a good thing in Rosie's eyes. She would like to keep school and her mum separate but it was a no-go area. Rosie carefully packed the letters away into her bag and studied her timetable cautiously. She was in set one or two for most of her subjects, apart from English, which she was really bad at. This meant separation from Flora and Daisy, who were pretty good at everything. Set three for English also meant Mr Atwood, which Rosie had heard was not good. She groaned and showed the girls her timetable.

'Oh, he's not so bad. My sister had him when she was in Year Ten. She said you just have to get him talking about his spaniels and his shooting weekends with his friends and he'll be off for hours talking about the good old days,' Flora informed Rosie. 'Don't worry. Anyway, you know who else'll be in your set, don't you? Tartan McFartan!' Flora and Daisy dissolved into high-pitched giggles as they saw the look on Rosie's face.

How had they worked it out? She had been trying

to keep it a secret for most of Year Seven. She thought she'd been successful. Rosie could feel herself blushing furiously as she tried to deny liking Toby McGregor. Why they couldn't just say his name properly she didn't know. It just made matters worse that they had given him a nickname and now Miss Wilde was coming over to find out what all the fuss was about. She shouted at them in front of the rest of the form.

'You are supposed to be packing up to go to assembly. *Not* wetting yourselves like primary school kids! Sort yourselves out, girls, *for goodness' sake*!'

She was in a seriously bad mood. Shouting at them had made her go bright red in the face. All her hair grips were falling out as she marched them over to the door.

'For your information I don't like him any more,' Rosie muttered under her breath as they trooped off to the assembly hall. 'I fancy someone else now, so you can both shut up and stop calling him that stupid name – you are *soooo* immature.'

This denial only made them laugh all the more. Daisy got out her compact mirror to show Rosie just how red she had gone. When she did Rosie got the shock of her life. She had been expecting to see her face all red, flushed, embarrassed and cross but what she saw instead was that her hair looked as if it were on fire. Her face in comparison looked quite normal to her.

'You've gone bright red, Rosie! You are totally in lurve with Jock the Scot. There's no way you've gone off him. As if!'

Flora looked delighted with their discovery. Daisy offered Rosie her foundation to cover up her redness and Miss Wilde shoved them through the door to join the rest of the class, who were already in the hall. Rosie didn't have time to look in the mirror again as it had been confiscated along with Daisy's make-up bag by Miss Wilde, much to Daisy's annoyance. Rosie didn't have time to process what had happened. Even if she had had time, she wasn't sure she'd be able to work out what was going on inside or outside her head. It felt as if she had pins and needles all over the top of her head. She rubbed at her scalp, hoping to stop the tingly sensation, and decided that whatever it was would have to wait until later.

After assembly it had been back to the form room to talk about the new school year and everything that would be expected from them now they were no longer in Year Seven. It turned out that rather a lot would be expected from them. Most of it was fairly tedious but there was one saving grace, they were going to have Year Captains. One boy and one girl were going to be chosen from each year as representatives. Rosie was quite keen on applying for the post herself. Whoever got voted in would be in charge of organising the lower school events, such as the charity disco for the NSPCC this year. Rosie, Flora and Daisy all raised their eyebrows and grinned at each other when this was mentioned.

Rosie knew the other two wouldn't be interested in running for Year Captain but hoped they would help her out with a campaign. Voting was in one month's time. She wouldn't have long to sort herself out. By break time Rosie's stomach was grumbling, but the pins-and-needles sensation in her head had died down a little.

They had spent all of lesson one and some of lesson two sorting out problems with timetables and uniforms and other boring stuff. To make matters worse they were then sent off for the last part of lesson two, which was, unfortunately for Rosie, English with Mr Atwood. The girls had arranged to meet in the toilets by the canteen at break. This was where Rosie was headed when she bumped into Toby McGregor coming out of the canteen queue, swigging out of a carton. When Rosie looked up, she saw that their collision had caused Toby to spill his chocolate milk-shake all down his clean white shirt.

'Oh my God! I am *so* sorry. I didn't see you. Oh, look at your shirt. Let me get that off . . .'

Rosie found herself automatically leaning forward to wipe his shirt. She stopped herself in horror, realising just in time that she wasn't his mum or his girlfriend and should really leave before she made matters worse.

As she flung herself into the sanctuary of the girls' toilets she could hear Toby's mates taking the mickey out of him and her. The words 'idiot' and 'klutz' and other unkind phrases followed her in as the door swung shut.

Rosie sighed and fought her way through the crowd, which was already three deep at the mirrors, looking for Daisy and Flora. She couldn't see them anywhere – typical, just when she really needed them. As usual, there was a huge queue for the cubicles, and Rosie decided she might as well join it while she was here. As she stood against the wall waiting her turn, Rosie glanced over to the sinks to see if she recognised anyone. It was mostly Year Nine and Ten girls.

Several were applying copious amounts of make-up while those further away from the all-important mirrors were chatting and gossiping and generally moaning about being back at school so soon.

The conversation consisted of spots, make-up and SATs or GCSEs. Now that they were sophisticated Year Nines and Tens they had serious exams to think of. Rosie sighed with relief that she was in Year Eight and didn't have that pressure just yet.

Rosie could feel her eyes blurring as she looked at the crowd of girls in front of her. Perhaps she was hungrier than she had thought. She often felt really dizzy lately if she didn't eat regularly. To make matters worse, the pins-and-needles feeling in her head had come back.

She rubbed her eyes and tried to refocus but it was getting more and more difficult to make out definite lines or shapes. What she appeared to be seeing instead was almost a mesh of . . . colours? Each person she looked at had a glow around them, but each person was a different colour or shade rather than a shape.

Rosie felt her forehead to see if she had a temperature, but it was cool to the touch – sort of damp, which Rosie thought wasn't good either. She could feel her breathing getting tighter in her chest. As she looked around the toilets trying to work out what was going on with her eyesight, she began to feel quite panicked and claustrophobic. Every girl she looked at was surrounded with a halo of colour, which seemed to range from reds and oranges to yellows to greens and sometimes purples. It felt as if she had got soap in her eyes, which she rubbed, hoping to clear her sight. She felt increasingly ill and out of control and desperately wanted to leave, but seemed almost paralysed. She couldn't tear her eyes or herself away from the colours and shapes in front of her.

When the drumming in her head began and the conversation and words of the girls mingled into one, Rosie began to panic. There must be something seriously wrong with her; this was not right. It was like the radio noise in the car on the way home from the holiday. All she could hear was static and buzzing. She knew she was going to faint and started to look for a way out.

Maybe she should go to the nurse's room. She began to feel shaky and sick and just as she was ready to collapse Daisy and Flora burst out of one of the cubicles and spotted Rosie in the queue. As soon as the three made eye contact Rosie sensed there was something wrong. It wasn't unusual for the girls to share a loo as it saved time – that wasn't what was bothering Rosie. What really troubled her was that before she even opened her mouth to try and tell the girls what had happened she saw that there was a red glow around the both of them. They looked as if they should be in a Ready Brek advert, where the little character is surrounded by red after he's eaten his heart-warming porridge.

Rosie, however, didn't feel heart-warmed. She put a hand to her ear, which was burning hot. Her head was pounding so soundly that she was certain it was about to explode. She still felt as if she had something in her eyes and couldn't see properly. And worst of all she was sure that they had been talking about her. For the first time in their lives, the girls all seemed at a loss for words. As the bell rang for lessons, Rosie stumbled blindly out of the toilets on legs that didn't work properly and found herself outside, being violently sick in the bushes.

☽ ★ Yellow ✳

Rosie made it to the nurse's room with the help of two Year Nine girls who had followed her out of the toilets and taken charge. She was instructed to rest on the couch until her mum came to pick her up.

'Right, madam,' said Rosie's mum as soon as they stepped into the house. 'Well, off to bed with you and no argument. I'll bring you some chicken soup later. Tess is going to sit with you this evening as I can't change my shift again. Whew! What a dramatic first day back. I wonder what brought this on? Well, you need fluids and plenty of them and we'll see how you are in the morning. I'm sure you'll be well enough for school – don't want to miss any more, do you?'

Rosie's mum tucked her into bed, patted her pillows and opened the skylight window a little as she chatted to Rosie in her nurse's voice. Rosie let her mum fuss and boss her around. She didn't have the energy to argue and she knew Tess would let her make a bed on the sofa and watch telly later on anyway. Rosie's mum was friendly with her neighbour Tess, who was recently divorced, and fond of Rosie. She often babysat if Rosie's mum was on a nightshift.

Perhaps because of the unusual afternoon nap Rosie couldn't sleep at all later that night. Eventually, after what felt like hours of turning over and huffing and puffing and flinging pillows and the duvet around her bed, she reached over and turned on her bedside lamp. Rosie decided to consult her favourite and most battered book to test her eyesight and also to see what it had to say about her condition.

Dr Star's Signs of the Times had been bought for Rosie by Flora and Daisy two Christmases ago and Rosie had almost read it cover to cover. There were sections she knew off by heart but there was one thing she had never looked up or consulted: colours and what people's star signs say about their colours. She turned to the index at the back and found two page references to colour. She read them quickly and found nothing useful apart from the word 'aura', which she'd heard of before but never fully explored.

The book told her to turn to page fifty-six if she wanted to know more, which after a day of seeing a multitude of colours, fuzziness and hearing strange whirring and buzzing noises she definitely did. Rosie was very concerned about the things that had happened to her. Weird did not begin to cover the day she'd had and there was no explanation she could think of to shed light on it all. Rosie read on:

> *An aura is a quality, an air, an atmosphere considered distinctive of a person or thing. It can often be seen as a shape around a person – as a colour or shade influencing a person or indicative of their mood.*

Mood. *Hmm, interesting*, thought Rosie, *that a colour can tell you how someone is feeling*. She continued reading the aura section and came across a colour chart which told her everything she needed to know:

> *There are three essential shades when studying someone's aura: red, yellow and green. Below is a chart explaining what each of these colours means with regards to mood and feeling. Although you may see an aura of other colours, it is these three dominant colours that are most revealing when reading auras.*

COLOUR	MOOD
Red	*Negative, angry, violent, lying, aggressive, passionate*
Yellow	*Unsure, uncertain, indecisive, jealous, indifferent*
Green	*Positive, happy, certain, honest, sure, safe, content*

In order for the mind to open and access someone's aura, you must allow yourself to relax, your eyes to lose focus on sharp objects and all sense of words and clear sounds to merge together to form a softer pattern of noise. Try to shut out the world around you and concentrate on an area just above the person's head, letting the colours flow and tell you all you need to know.

As she digested this information Rosie popped to the loo as she was still wide awake and wanted to check her vision again. After washing her hands she found herself looking in the mirror at her reflection for much longer than normal. She wasn't sure what she was hoping to find but she knew that the answers lay in the mirror. The more Rosie stared, the more she found herself searching for a colour, fuzziness, pins and needles – any of the things that had made her first day back at school so extraordinary.

For some unknown reason Rosie must have been able to see people's auras by seeing colours around them. That must have been what went on earlier that day. There was no another explanation . . . But why her and why now, and why did it make her feel so dizzy and sick?

Rosie suffered a sleepless night and as a result was not ready for her mum and an awkward breakfast interrogation the following morning. She was still trying to piece together the unusual events of the previous day and her mum chattering on in her ear wasn't helping her concentration at all.

'What's this nonsense about Year Captains? You're not going to run for this post, are you, Rosie? Don't you think you'd be better off concentrating on improving your English and trying to move up a set before half-term? You need to be in set one or two for Year Nine, so you stand a good chance in your exams. Are you feeling better? You look a bit peaky still. Maybe I should take you into work with me, but then I don't want you to miss out on . . .'

Rosie was struggling to remember if the cereal went in first, or the milk; and did she want just butter on her toast or jam too? These were difficult decisions to make when you've had approximately three hours' sleep. Struggling to lift her head to look at her mum, Rosie found herself drifting off into a daydream. It was one of her favourites, one where she lived on her own, in a penthouse apartment which had a diner around the corner called Barney's. Delicious breakfasts could be ordered and brought to her door with all the decisions made for her and without the presence of a noisy mother, full of questions about exams.

'I think I'd be a good Year Captain. I'm not moving English sets. I'm just no good at it. Sorry.'

This was a mammoth effort, but Rosie knew from years of experience that if she didn't say something her mum would simply continue her monologue undeterred, possibly for hours. Rosie had to get to school this morning and not only come up with her campaign for Year Captain but a plan to find out what was going on with Flora and Daisy. They seemed to be involved in this colour confusion too and under normal circumstances Rosie would have told them all about it and asked them to help her work it out. But they were up to something and, in any case, Rosie wasn't quite ready to tell them yet, especially when she didn't really know what to tell them. Maybe this new colour thing would come in handy, although she wasn't quite sure how. Maybe it would be better to keep it a secret, just for now.

Rosie felt her eyes were a lot better today, despite having hardly slept during the night. She could see the whiteboard clearly and everyone seemed much more in focus in English. She must have been ill yesterday and had a temperature and been hallucinating. That would explain it all much better than this aura business, which sounded most unlikely.

Silent reading was the most boring lesson on the planet and Mr Atkins was the most tedious teacher. It did, however, give Rosie time to come up with her plan of action for becoming Year Eight's Captain. Underneath the cover of the book she was pretending to read, she drew up a list of all the reasons people should vote for her:

Rosie Sallis for Year Captain!

1. I know almost everyone in the year as I went to primary school with them.
2. I get on with most people (apart from spoilt Princesses).
3. I am not a troublemaker but I will stand up for student rights.

4. My mum is on the PTA, so I get to find out about school stuff the same time as the teachers instead of ages later!

Rosie got stuck after number four and decided to put her list away to show Flora and Daisy later. They would be certain to have loads more reasons and ideas to help and maybe once they had sorted out her campaign they could sort out her eyesight and this colour chaos.

At lunchtime, Rosie waited impatiently for Flora and Daisy to come and sit down. They always took ages in the queue. Rosie had packed lunches as her mum knew she would eat chips and burgers if given the privilege of school dinners. Flora and Daisy's mums weren't really aware of the horrors of the school canteen and so her friends were given plenty of dinner money to spend on what they liked. This meant Rosie saved the table while Flora and Daisy feasted themselves on all kinds of fast food. Rosie opened her lunch box and was concentrating on unpacking her various items so that she didn't see Toby McGregor approach her table. Unfortunately as she looked up she had most of her peanut butter and jam sandwich hanging out of her mouth.

'Mfhhmnn.'

'Yeah, right, whatever. Anyway, I hear you're running for Year Captain for the girls, yeah?' Toby questioned her.

'Mmhhhmm.'

'I'm running for the boys, so maybe we should meet up and talk about campaigns and stuff, yeah? Sound! See ya!'

Flora and Daisy, who had been stood excitedly behind Toby, sat down, both grinning madly at Rosie, who was furiously chewing away at her sandwich unable to answer Toby as he wandered off to his mates' table.

'What did he want? Was he asking you out? Was he asking about me?' Flora began excitedly.

'No! He's running for Captain for the boys and wanted to get together to talk about campaigns. Who knows where that could lead, well, if I ever manage to empty my mouth and speak to him? Gross! I am never having these sandwiches again! How embarrassing. I couldn't speak; the peanut butter practically welded my mouth together! Why would you think he was asking about you? Anyway on to more important business . . .'

Rosie decided this was the perfect opportunity to

divert attention from her disastrous moment with Toby and show the girls her list. As they read through it Rosie watched them carefully, remembering yesterday and their odd behaviour in the girls' toilets.

'Well, not bad, Rose,' said Flora, looking up at her, then at Daisy, 'but to be honest I think you need something a bit more . . . well, *dynamic*, if you're going to beat the competition.'

'What competition? Do you know who else is running? I bet it's Rebecca O'Farrell; she and her Princess club think they are "it",' Rosie muttered, and they all cast Rebecca's table their most filthy looks.

Rebecca O'Farrell was Rosie's chief enemy at school as she had gone out with Toby in Year Seven and had never let Rosie forget it, even though Toby dumped her over the summer. Rebecca was a Princess and her table of friends her loyal courtiers. Rosie, Flora and Daisy avoided them like the plague. Once Rosie was satisfied with the filthy looks she had dished out to Rebecca she turned her attention back to her real friends, and as she did so, she caught Daisy and Flora looking at each other with guilty looks. *Not again*, thought Rosie. *This is becoming a nasty habit.*

Daisy definitely looked shifty and refused to meet Rosie's gaze, so Rosie decided to concentrate and let her eyes go blurry in an attempt to experiment with the whole colour thing. She felt the pins and needles start up in her feet instantly. Around Daisy's neat brown hair was an orangey red glow. *There is definitely something going on here*, Rosie thought, and as she felt her stomach turn over she regretted eating her sandwiches.

Flora's hair seemed even redder than Daisy's, which was odd as she was blonde. They were keeping a secret from her, Rosie was certain, and the colours around their heads simply confirmed this for her! What she now had to work out was what the secret was and why.

'What? What are you up to? Are you planning a campaign for me? A surprise? I know you're up to something. What is it? Come on . . .'

Flora took a deep breath, looked at Daisy, who nodded, and began to explain.

'Sorry, Rosie, but *I'm* your competition. I decided yesterday that I wanted to go for Year Captain and I asked Daisy to be my manager. We didn't know you wanted to go for it, too. But why don't you join me and you can be my assistant or something?'

'Oh . . . how generous of you, Flora. I don't *want* to be your assistant. Toby is going to be the boys'

Captain and I *have* to be the girls'. You knew I'd go for it! How could you? It's my only chance with him and you're going to ruin it for me!'

Rosie was so angry. The girls had never really argued before. Not over something serious anyway. Before Daisy could fulfil her role as the peacemaker, Rosie stormed off. Flora was left looking guilty with her red glow and Daisy, panicked, was surrounded by a wobbly orange glimmer.

The argument had made Rosie even more determined to win this battle. The added incentive of Toby McGregor being the boys' Captain was merely the icing on the cake. There was no way on earth she was letting Flora steal her thunder and possibly a lot more. Flora was already one of the most popular girls at school; she was very confident, pretty and clever. Liked by everyone, she already had so much, thought Rosie, it was greedy and unfair of Flora to ask for more. She always seemed to know what to say and when to say it, whereas Rosie often ended up putting her foot in her mouth – or a huge peanut butter and jam sandwich, just at the wrong moment!

There had to be a way to use this new-found power to her advantage. Rosie wasn't sure how just yet, but she would find out and soon. There was no time to lose here, she decided as she looked in the bathroom mirror later that night, brushing her teeth. This colour thing was going to help her. But first she had to try it out and get the hang of it at home, on her own.

She concentrated hard and let her eyes go fuzzy, watching as her reflection lost its sharp edges and lines and became softer, taking on a yellow hue. The pins and needles felt more familiar and less painful, and her eyes seemed to focus in on colour a lot quicker than they did yesterday. She definitely didn't feel sick, wobbly or claustrophobic, which was a huge improvement. She consulted *Dr Star's Signs of the Times*, and reread the meaning of a yellow aura, which was the colour surrounding her in the mirror.

Unsure, uncertain, indecisive or jealous.

Well, she was feeling all of those emotions – so this aura awareness must really mean something. There was no other reasonable explanation that could account for Rosie seeing colours around people when she had never done before. It had started soon after she had been to Florien's Fates and Fortunes tent at the fair. But how could spending a few minutes in an old tent with a complete stranger make Rosie, a completely normal person, see auras? All for a fiver?

It seemed a little unlikely, but then Rosie had no other explanation for all the weird things that had been happening to her ever since her visit to the fair.

The first time must have been in the car on the way home. She had felt sick, had pins and needles, couldn't see properly, heard buzzing sounds, and then there was the traffic light thing. She had thought the traffic lights were on red but that must have been the colour around her mum's head . . . which must mean that she was lying, or keeping something from her? What exactly was she doing while Rosie was on the rides? And why did she suddenly agree to let her go to the fair? This was getting more and more complicated.

So far her life had been the complete opposite of weird, unusual or exciting. It was time she got spiritual and different and learned to live life by the seat of her pants – just like her grandpa was always saying he used to! Rosie had always wondered what he meant by that. Well, perhaps now she'd find out. No more regular, boring Rosie. No one wanted to vote for a boring Year Captain. She needed an advantage to swing the vote her way, and away from the competition, her ex-best friend!

Rosie wanted more proof of her new gift, so she

ventured downstairs to watch TV with her mum. If this was not going to work on anyone, it would be her. She didn't believe in star signs, clairvoyants, psychics or fortune-tellers, let alone auras. She was Mrs Sensible and therefore the best person to try this out on.

Rosie's mum, having been at work all day, would be fairly easy to read. Knowing her mum and what she was like at the end of the day, Rosie guessed her mum's aura would be reddish. Red meant *'angry, violent, lying, aggressive, passionate'*. She was bound to be a little angry mixed in with passionate. Her job always made her feel this way, and, unfortunately for Rosie, all too often her bad mood spilled over into her home life. Rosie normally avoided her mum for at least half an hour before approaching her, especially if she wanted something. Tonight, however, was special; Rosie wanted something entirely different from her mum.

After sitting next to her on the sofa for thirty minutes and concentrating very hard, Rosie had a good idea how to use the auras to her advantage in more ways than one. Perhaps the fiver spent at Florien's Fates and Fortunes wasn't a complete waste of money.

Green

The thought of going to school the next day was exciting. Rosie couldn't wait to try out her newly acquired talent on her friends and maybe some of the teachers. Mr McCabe and Miss Wilde would be her first targets. Flora had suspicions about their form tutor and the history teacher and now it was time to put her theories to the test.

Miss Wilde was in a bad mood again. She had crashed her car into the back of someone at a round-about that morning and was in no mood for chatting or laughter of any kind. She was very much in the mood for silent reading and passing the time standing out in the hallway, shouting into her mobile phone at a garage and then at her insurance company – a private conversation that the whole class was engrossed in. It was so entertaining to hear a teacher swear when they didn't think anyone was listening.

Rosie had forgotten her library books, so she had to resort to doing her maths homework, which was failing to hold her attention. She found herself tuning into Miss Wilde's conversation instead, which, despite taking place out in the hall, was very easy to hear.

'For goodness' sake! I've told you it wasn't my fault. The way was clear, no one was coming and he should have pulled out, so I had to slam my breaks on . . . What? Well, yes *I did* because the way was clear. It doesn't matter, does it? So because *I* got stuck behind someone who should have had their licence taken off them centuries ago, I lose out on my insurance, do I? Right, right, well, *thank you*! Thank you very much for *nothing*!'

Rosie wasn't interested in insurance companies as she didn't really understand half of what Miss Wilde was on about. But what was becoming clear was that Miss Wilde was lying. Rosie knew this for certain because she had wandered out into the hallway to pretend to look at the noticeboard and could see Miss Wilde clearly. She had an unmistakable red colour all around her short brown hair, which was spiky and standing on end. It looked as if she had pulled chunks of it out in her frustration. Rosie poked her head back into the classroom and could see watery colours outlining the heads of all her classmates. The colours seemed to change as the seconds went by for some people; others stayed the same. Rosie supposed it depended on what they were thinking or feeling as they read their books and magazines and secretly texted boyfriends and girlfriends.

This was mind-blowing. It was like being in a secret world where she could tap into what people were really feeling and thinking without them knowing it. She had always been interested in her own future, but there was always so much to think about that day, let alone the next week, month or year. Now she felt she had been given a gift which would help her make all the right choices and decisions and maybe help others, too.

Time to try it out! Rosie approached Miss Wilde's desk as her teacher threw herself into her chair, having slammed the classroom door shut behind her. Rosie was keen to see how her aura might tell her more about the car crash.

'Sorry to hear about your accident, miss. Poor you. Was it road rage?'

Rosie put on her most sympathetic face. Good job no one could read *her* aura as they would know she was lying. She thought Miss Wilde was a moany old cow and deserved what she got.

'Yes, well, there are some *real idiots* on the road, unfortunately for me!'

Rosie tried to look subtly at Miss Wilde's face and hairline as she concentrated on writing a note at her desk. It was quite green, so she must be telling the truth; well, yeah, Rosie knew there were idiots on the road – her mum said as much frequently – but Rosie wondered if Miss Wilde was one of them.

'As you're here you can do me a favour, Rosie. Take this note about next week's assemblies to Mr McCabe, please. He's in H3.'

Rosie noticed that as Miss Wilde folded the note her aura changed from a green shade to a flaming red one. Rosie waited until she was out of sight of their tutor room before opening the note and reading it.

Sean, can you take me home later? Had stupid car crash this morning. Some old man's fault – not mine! Need lots of wine and TLC tonight. Luv Jen xxx

Well, this was seriously interesting news. Rosie couldn't wait until she got back to the tutor room to tell Flora and Daisy all about what had to be the juiciest teacher-related gossip so far this term. Flora had been saying for the last year that there was something going on between Miss Wilde and Mr McCabe. Daisy and Rosie had thought she was nuts and had been watching too many soaps, but it appeared she had been right all along. Rosie then remembered that she wasn't talking to Flora. Well, she would just share her majorly massive information with Daisy and Flora could suffer! That would teach her. Trying to steal Toby from under Rosie's eyes was not something she was prepared to forgive or forget easily.

As Rosie knocked on the door of H3 her stomach turned over, as it inevitably did when she thought of Toby. He was in Mr McCabe's tutor group and Rosie was glad to deliver the note as it gave her a chance to see him AND, she suddenly realised, Mr McCabe's aura too! Rosie had to firmly switch her mind back to the main reason she was here, the romance of the school! She wondered what Mr McCabe's aura would tell her as he read the note. Being able to read people's true emotions was making her life much more entertaining and enlightening.

'Sorry to interrupt, sir. I've got a note from Miss Wilde for you.'

Rosie eagerly handed the note over and watched as Mr McCabe read on, making sure that she kept her eyes on the teacher and not on Toby. Mr McCabe pulled a serious looking face as he wrote his reply on a clean piece of paper, carefully putting Miss Wilde's note in his pocket for safe keeping.

'There you go. Thanks, ermm, Rosemary.'

Rosie rolled her eyes; he never got her name right. She decided now was the time to push her luck and test her skills again.

'Um, Miss Wilde said it was about the assemblies next week. Are you taking one, sir?'

Mr McCabe looked confused for a moment and then regained control. As he replied Rosie watched with interest as his forehead took on an orangey glow.

'Yes, I'm doing an assembly on um . . . on Wednesday actually, so don't be late! HA! Ha! Hmm, right, Rosemary. Well, you'd better get back to Miss Wilde.'

Rosie stole a quick glance at Toby as she left the tutor room. He had his head buried in what looked like a surfing magazine and hadn't even noticed her. Rosie shrugged her disappointment off as she read the note while walking back to her form room. It still amazed her that teachers thought pupils wouldn't read their notes. There was no way Rosie would trust anyone in Year Eight to carry a note for her! Well, she might have trusted Flora once, but not any more. Mr McCabe was clearly more trusting than she was.

J, that's fine. I'll see you in the staffroom at lunch. Sx

Women definitely wrote better notes than men. This was such a boring reply and gave nothing away, but Rosie didn't need the note to know how Mr McCabe felt; she had seen the colours painted on his face – real passion! Why he felt passion for Miss Wilde was beyond Rosie, yet there was no arguing with the facts. Now she had evidence and had proved to herself that she could read auras, it was time for some fun in technicolour.

Orange

Break time was the most important time of day at school. It was when everyone got together and gossiped about whoever was flavour of the day, or not as the case may be. Rosie knew she had something of great interest to tell everyone and was picking her moment to drop her gossip bomb. She knew that not just people in Year Eight would be interested in her news, but the whole school. Something like this was huge and she wanted to get credit for it.

Rosie positioned herself in the canteen between the Princesses' table, where Rebecca was holding court, and the Year Ten prefects, who were trying to manage the queue, which was quickly becoming a rugby scrum. Rosie decided to go for volume over detail and simply came out with her newsflash at the top of her voice.

'Guess who is going out with Mr McCabe? Miss Wilde!'

Rosie had everyone's attention and as more people

gathered around she repeated herself and embellished with the scandalous details of the unsuspecting teachers' notes. Rosie observed with satisfaction as the Chinese whispers started and quickly circulated around the canteen. She felt pleased with herself and very important as a few people came up to her to check their information with her, the source. It was slightly disturbing that some people were asking when the baby was due and did Rosie know that Mr McCabe and Miss Wilde had already got secretly married in the Caribbean this summer? Well, whatever the rumours had now grown into, this was the romance of the school and she had found out about it! It was amazing what little effort it had taken and the attention she was getting as a result was more than worthwhile.

It was important to understand that Mr McCabe was not good-looking in the usual sense, but inside the world of school, in comparison to the other male teachers, he was thought of as fairly fit. The fact that Miss Wilde was not exactly cover-girl material didn't matter; in fact, it made the relationship even more intriguing. The topic of Mr McCabe's girlfriend and whether he had one was of relevance to most Year Eight, Nine and Ten girls and had been for some time.

Rosie had hoped that this newly acquired skill would come in useful, but had no idea that it was going to make her popular and cool, or that she would be able to impress people who normally wouldn't look twice at her with such ease.

As the crowd grew and the volume challenged that of a football stadium Rosie knew there was no way she could now tell Daisy or Flora about her seeing auras. This was something she was going to have to keep to herself. They just wouldn't believe her or understand. Rosie watched with a sense of smugness as Flora went off to the toilets on her own for once, leaving Daisy at Rosie's side. Rosie was, without a doubt, the centre of attention this break time.

Dr Star's Signs of the Times normally held the answers for Rosie. but tonight there was nothing in there that would help her. This was a solo project. She couldn't even ask the fortune-teller for advice as the fair would have moved on by now and she had no way of finding out where they had gone. There must be a reason why this thing had happened to her, it couldn't just be luck; but like luck, Rosie felt there would come a point when it would run out, so it was time to take advantage and use it to get what she wanted . . . Toby. Of course, being elected to Year

Captain wasn't to be sniffed at either. Plan A needed to be put into action:

Plan A
Use auras to work out what people really think about school, find out what they want to happen at school and then give it to them.

Plan B
Find out what Toby thinks of me and Princess Rebecca. Find out what he likes in a girl and what his interests are, then become knowledgeable about them all and impress him with my charm and intelligence, even if I have to learn about surfing and car engines.

The first opportunity Rosie got to put her aura-seeing eyes to use was Charity Day. They had several every year at school; for one pound they could wear what they wanted for the day and at lunchtime there would be some form of activity to raise even more money. The money went to a different charity each time. The idea had been Rosie's mum's when her hospital needed funds for a new ward, and it had stuck. Rosie didn't tell anyone it was her mum's idea, but was secretly proud of her.

This time the charity was the RSPCA and the lunchtime event in the main dinner hall was a debate. Rosie signed herself up. She needed to be seen as a 'joiner'; she needed to make herself visible to the rest of the year so that when it came to voting time people would actually know who she was. The topics were secret, so they couldn't prepare, which didn't bother Rosie until she found out her opponent was Flora. Miss Wilde had a nasty streak in her and knew they weren't talking over the Year Captaincy thing. She had clearly thought it would be very funny to pit them against each other in the charity debate. Funny, ha ha! Well, maybe it would be funnier than Rosie thought, now that she had all the colours of the rainbow on her side.

The debate was packed out. There wasn't much to do at lunchtime in school as going into town was out of bounds to lower school. Rosie was beginning to get nervous. She had tried to persuade Toby to join in, too, not just because of the elections but because it gave her an excuse to talk to him. He wasn't remotely interested but had promised to be watching Rosie from the floor.

The Year Seven kids went first: their topics were the environment, vegetarians and animal testing –

easy ones, Rosie thought as she listened half-heartedly while maintaining her vow of silence with Flora, who was trying to smile at her across the stage.

Rosie and Flora were next for Year Eight. As they approached their lecterns, Ian Summers, Head Boy, handed them their cards, hit the gong and told them their time had started. Rosie ripped open her envelope, pulled the card out and read aloud, '*The class system – against.*'

Great, thought Rosie. She wasn't even sure what the class system was, other than the lectures her mum had given her on class over the years and that she was from working-class stock, as her grandpa proudly informed her. Well, Flora definitely wasn't working class and she was arguing for a class system. Flora began her opening statement.

'I believe there is still a class system in our country and that everyone secretly knows what class they are. It depends on your job, income, home and area in which you live, but it's not just about material possessions; it's also a feeling of where you are in the world, your place and role in society . . .'

Flora was giving out a green glow as she ranted on and on about things she had clearly heard at home; she sounded just like her mum. She obviously believed in what she was saying as her aura was a distinct green. By the time Flora had finished speaking, Rosie had worked out what to say.

'Without wishing to state the obvious . . . there *is* no class system any more. There are not many grammar schools left; anyone can go to a school and get a decent education and anyone can go to Oxford or Cambridge now if they want. Not that *I* would, as they are snobby and posh, but it's the principal of the thing. Not everyone is obsessed with earning loads of money and having a flash car and a big house and all of that material rubbish; some people are more concerned about the real issues. I don't think there is such a thing as working, middle or upper class. I think people are just people who have different kinds of jobs and earn different kinds of money and there are no class labels any more. The only people interested in class are the so-called "upper class" so that they can smugly label themselves and think that they are superior to everyone else.'

Rosie hadn't really thought through what she was saying but she could see Flora getting crosser as she carried on. Just as they were getting into the argument, Ian Summers interrupted and gave Flora one point, took their cards away and gave them new ones.

Each pair got three topics each and it was the best of three that decided the winner.

Rosie was hoping for something that she knew about this time around and she was relieved to find they were talking on a subject she felt strongly about. She couldn't help wondering how much of a hand Miss Wilde may have had in choosing the debate topics.

Star signs – for

Rosie began this time.

'Star signs have been around for a long, long time and everyone from me to the Queen likes reading their stars in the paper and magazines. There are thousands of websites on them and you can even get your star-sign forecast for the year ahead made up for you if you know where and when you were born.

'Star signs have been proven right many times: just look at Nostradamus and his predictions – lots of those have come true. For example, I can tell you are an Aries, Flora. All Aries are fiery and bad tempered, aren't they? All Aries are also competitive and greedy and want to have everything for themselves, whereas Virgos are much more chilled and peaceful. Star signs tell us a lot about people's characters, it's just some people don't like hearing the truth.'

Flora was trying hard not to swear as she gave her reply. She had lost the smug green colour from the previous argument and was doing a good impression of a bubbling volcano about to erupt with red lava everywhere.

'What a load of rubbish, Rosie. No one with a logical mind believes in star signs. They are just something to pacify people who can't think for themselves. Star signs are written to reassure people who need others to tell them what they are like and what kind of character they have. Well, I can tell you what kind of character people who believe in star signs have: no character. They are spineless believers in fairytales.'

Wow, the gloves were definitely off now. This was clearly nothing less than war. The gong sounded and Ian awarded Rosie the point and told Flora to watch her language. Rosie scanned the growing crowd quickly and noticed that in the sea of colours the one that stood out most was yellow. She and Flora were confusing the crowd. The next argument had to be hers; a lot more than Charity Day depended on this. If she won the debate people would be more likely to vote for her as Year Eight Year Captain. Rosie knew Flora would be thinking the same. The last topic they were given had a lot depending on it. Rosie opened her envelope cautiously and read:

Best friends – against

Rosie then knew that her Head of Year *must* have chosen the topics. Miss Wilde had clearly not got rid of her evil mood and was trying to provoke them into a real argument, or perhaps, in her own freakish way, was trying to get them to make up? Who knew? Luckily for Rosie it was Flora's turn to begin. They had one point each: this argument would be the decider, and not just of the debate.

'Best Friends are really important for people, especially when you are at school, as they can stick up for you. They know what you like and dislike, they are there for you when things are going badly and when things are going well and everyone should have one. A true best friend can forgive and forget and knows how and when to make up and when to admit they were in the wrong. A real best friend is a friend for life.'

Well, there were so many messages and codes in there, Rosie was thrown for a moment. She nearly took Flora's advice and was thinking of forgiving her, but then she remembered the motivating factor behind their argument, Toby McGregor, and changed her mind. Rosie searched the crowd for Toby, located him, and gave him a winning smile as she attempted to give a winning speech.

'I agree to a certain point that best friends are important, etc., but not when they become bad friends; friends who go behind your back, who take other friends off you, who lie to you. That's not a friend, it's an enemy. If you only have best friends at school, when you fall out with them you'll then be left on your own at break and lunch, so I think you should have a large group of different friends, for different occasions and leave best friends where they belong – in primary school!'

Lots of people seemed to agree with this in the audience as Rosie noticed a green colour descend over the heads of most of Year Seven and Eight, who were always falling out with best friends, arguing and then making up again. Year Nine looked less sure, forming a custard yellow group at the back. Flora definitely didn't agree and was turning an attractive shade of tomato, shaking her head angrily at Rosie. Ian had a quick discussion with Jude Cheek, the Head Girl, and stepped forward to the microphone. Rosie held her breath. She desperately wanted to win and she knew Flora would be feeling just the same. Rosie crossed her fingers and silently prayed, even though she only believed in God when she wanted something.

'Well, that was the liveliest discussion so far. Cheers, ladies. OK, so the winner is . . . both of you. It's a tie. You both argued well. So well done, Year Eight. Now can the Year Nine candidates step forward, please? Girls . . . erm . . . you can leave the stage.'

Rosie and Flora looked at each other, preparing to grimace and scowl, but instead they ended up grinning at one another. Typical! A tie! Daisy came rushing up to them as they stepped off the stage.

'You were great, both of you. Everyone is saying you should both be Year Captains. Maybe you should do it together?'

Daisy quite often came up with the best ideas because they were simple. Why they hadn't thought of sharing it before now was clear – because they were both stubborn. Rosie looked at Flora, who nodded in agreement. Sometimes Rosie didn't need an aura to know what people were thinking. Well, not when it came to her best friend.

'I wasn't after Toby, you know, honestly,' Flora said. 'I know how much you like him. You should just get on with it and find out if he likes you back. Come on, I bet if we catch Miss Wilde when she's in a good mood and ask her she'll let us.'

They were all laughing hysterically at the prospect of Miss Wilde being in a good mood, when Rosie got her first really good idea about how to use her auras. Miss Wilde and Mr McCabe were going to be the first lucky people to be on the receiving end of Rosie's all-seeing aura eyes, they just didn't know it yet!

★ Emerald ✳

The whole school seemed to know about the big romance between Miss Wilde and Mr McCabe, who in turn seemed blissfully unaware of the public nature of their relationship. Clearly no student had been brave enough to ask Miss Wilde any questions about it yet. As for Mr McCabe, he was always off in his own world with the Romans or the Tudors. His passion for history made it quite hard to pin him down to the present and ask him much about this century, let alone his private life. History seemed to be his life – well, certainly in school time anyway.

Rosie had generously decided to give Miss Wilde the benefit of the doubt about the debate set-up and her carefully chosen topics. Rosie needed to concentrate on more serious matters, like getting her and Mr McCabe to admit their feelings for each other and let the school enjoy their romance. Maybe it would make Miss Wilde a better person if her secret were out in the open and she didn't have to sneak around and send stupid notes.

Tutor time on Friday morning gave Rosie her first opportunity to interrogate Miss Wilde, using her aura as a true guidance. Flora and Daisy still didn't know about Rosie's newly acquired talent. Rosie wasn't sure why she hadn't told them but she just had a feeling it would be better to leave it for a while. Flora might not understand and they were only just back to being friends; Rosie didn't want to spoil things.

Rosie had positioned herself at Miss Wilde's desk, offering her services as a board cleaner. Miss Wilde had spider's writing and tended to use the whole of the whiteboard in her lessons. As a result it was always covered with her messy sprawl and needed a good clean after every lesson. While Miss Wilde carried on with what looked like very boring marking, Rosie began her questions. Rosie knew her form tutor would be somewhat cagey, as the woman was always wary when students were friendly to her, but with the knowledge she was gaining daily from reading people's auras Rosie felt confident she could break through Miss Wilde's shell. She began with some casual questioning.

'So what are you doing at the weekend, then, miss? Got any plans?'

'Erm . . . seeing some friends. We might go to the cinema tonight. Why?'

'Just asking, miss. Making conversation. So would it be a chick flick you'd go and see, you know like a real girls' night out?'

Miss Wilde was too busy trying to get through an extraordinarily large pile of Year Ten exercise books to notice Rosie's persistence and answered without thinking.

'No, probably some action thriller. You know what men are like – it's got to have fighting and big explosions in it to be any good.'

Rosie decided to take advantage of this slip-up.

'So is it a date, then? Have you got a boyfriend, miss? You never mentioned him before.'

Miss Wilde realised her error too late and had to resort to what Rosie knew was a lie because of the telltale change in aura from emerald to a raving red.

'No, I have not. Not that it's any of your business. Have you finished cleaning my board yet? Go and sit down, please. For goodness' sake! Is there no privacy in this place?'

The last bit was muttered under her breath but Rosie caught it as she sat down, giving Flora and Daisy the thumbs-up and a wink. They would have to wait until the bell rang for first lesson before Rosie could give them a debriefing.

In the end they had to wait until break time to hear what Rosie had managed to find out. Flora and Daisy descended upon Rosie, who was waiting for them to leave the snacks queue.

'So, what did she say? Did you get any details?' Daisy demanded as she shoved an ice bun in her mouth. Daisy was the last of the great romantics and believed in soul mates and all that. Rosie and Flora weren't so sure. Unless Toby McGregor ever decided to ask her out, Rosie would reserve her judgement on soul mates.

'Well, they are going to the cinema together tonight to see some action film. So if we get the paper and find out what's on we could turn up and see the truth for ourselves. We could casually pop over and say hi, then they'll have to come out in the open and tell everyone.'

Rosie was really pleased with herself and her plan. Flora, however, spotted one fatal flaw.

'Just one problem, Rosie. There's no way they'll go to the cinema in town, as that's where we all go. They'll go somewhere else, won't they, and how are we supposed to find out where?'

Flora had a very good point, which was annoying, as Rosie hadn't thought of that. But she was determined not to be put off.

'Well, I'll just have to find out where they go and then we could get one of our parents to drive us there.'

'How are you going to find that out? There's no way she'll tell you that, and if you ask her she'll be on to you.' Flora had little faith in Rosie's detective skills but then she didn't know about the auras.

'Don't worry. I'll get it out of her before the end of the day,' Rosie replied confidently, and changed the subject to vital matters, such as what they were going to wear to the cinema.

By lunchtime Rosie had formulated her plan. She had decided to work on Mr McCabe instead; he was bound to be less cagey than Miss Wilde – the fact that Toby McGregor was in Mr McCabe's tutor group had nothing to do with it.

Mr McCabe was a history teacher and therefore knew about every famous speech that had ever been written, probably. To enter into the competition to become Year Captain students had to write a two-minute speech explaining why they would make a good candidate, which was a tiresome but necessary evil. Rosie decided to rely upon her feminine charms and flutter her eyelashes at Mr McCabe and ask for help and inspiration with her speech. She found him in his tutor room, marking. It would seem that all these teachers wanted to do was sit and mark books.

'Sorry to disturb you, sir, but I was wondering if you could help me with my speech for Year Captain. I know that there's that good one by Martin Luther King and a few others that I thought might help . . .'

Mr McCabe looked woefully at his pile of coursework and back at Rosie. She quickly took in his aura before listening to his reply.

'I'd love to help, Rosemary, but as you can see I've got all this Year Eleven coursework to mark for this afternoon.'

As he was the colour of a satsuma and therefore presumably lying, Rosie took a gamble.

'But you don't teach Year Eleven this afternoon, do you, sir? I thought you taught Year Eight, your tutor group?'

Rosie had obsessively memorised Toby's timetable in the hope of running into him outside rooms, accidentally. It therefore came in handy to know that he had Mr McCabe on a Friday afternoon. This knowledge, combined with his aura, told Rosie he was lying.

'Oh yeah, so I do. Must have got my timetable muddled up. How *clever* of you to remember. Well, it looks like I can help you, quickly, then.'

He looked a bit cross to start with but that soon changed once he got on to the topic of his hero, Martin Luther King, and his 'I have a dream' speech. Rosie took some of it in, as it was quite useful, especially the bit Mr McCabe read out in his very best actor's voice. It wasn't an impression of Martin Luther King but it was a very good 'speech voice' and Rosie was suitably impressed as Mr McCabe's voice resounded powerfully across the classroom.

'*And so even though we face the difficulties of today and tomorrow, I still have a dream. It is a dream deeply rooted in the American dream.*

'*I have a dream that one day this nation will rise up and live out the true meaning of its creed: "We hold these truths to be self-evident, that all men are created equal."*

'. . . *I have a dream that my four little children will one day live in a nation where they will not be judged by the colour of their skin but by the content of their character.*

'*I have a* dream *today!*'

As Mr McCabe came to the end of the speech, some of which he seemed to know almost off by heart, Rosie was thinking she had to find a way to work cinemas and Miss Wilde into the conversation. This wasn't easy when they were talking about one of the most important historic events of the twentieth century.

'So, sir, have you seen that really good film *Malcolm X*? He was very similar to Martin Luther King, wasn't he? He made some good speeches, too. I went to see it with my mum. It wasn't on at all the cinemas, you know. Did you see it?' Rosie knew he would have, she just had to get him to reveal where.

'Yes, I did. I saw it at the I-M cinema. They always show a wide range of films that some of the others don't. I'm surprised you enjoyed it – it's quite heavy. It was very moving, wasn't it? Maybe we could use some of Malcolm X's finer points in your speech. It would certainly give you an edge. I didn't realise you were so political, Rosemary.'

Rosie bit down on her tongue and managed not to scream out her proper name at him. He had given her the information she needed. She observed Mr McCabe's aura change from a suspicious satsuma shade to a more honest apple colour. Yes, he was telling the truth. Now all she had to do was find Daisy and Flora and arrange a lift quickly to the I-M cinema for tonight.

Rosie knew she was being obsessive about Mr McCabe and Miss Wilde and that others would have given up trying to prove a romance was going on between them by now. But there was more to it than that.

Rosie wanted real solid, concrete proof that her aura skills were not in her head. She needed to know that she was reading the auras correctly and putting this new-found skill to good use. She also wanted to check her romance-reading skills before trying to sort her own love life out, or rather lack of one. She only had until Christmas to get working on Toby. If he didn't ask her to the Christmas Charity Ball then she had decided to give up on him. But until then she needed every little bit of help she could get.

☽ ★ Sunshine ✳

Rosie's mum was working the day shift this week, so she volunteered to take them to the I-M cinema. There was something she wanted to watch herself – some Jane Austen film. It was bound to have lots of women in frilly dresses and bonnets and men in stupidly tight riding trousers, muttering on about taking 'a turn about the room'. Rosie declined her mum's offer of accompanying her to this evening of culture. She instead chose to watch the big action blockbuster on in screen three with Flora and Daisy, and hopefully Miss Wilde and Mr McCabe. She couldn't be sure that this was the cinema they would be going to, or that they would definitely be going tonight, but it was worth a try. She had to find proof of her skills somewhere and this seemed the best place to start.

They arrived in plenty of time for the all-important choosing of pick-and-mix sweets. For once, Rosie's mum hadn't moaned at them about their teeth. She had even paid for all of them to get huge bags full of

E-numbers and artificial flavourings, which was immensely satisfying.

Rosie's mum's film started before theirs, so she agreed to meet them in the foyer later. This left Rosie, Flora and Daisy free to look out for their teachers.

'Look!' hissed Daisy. She pointed to the main entrance, where Mr McCabe was waiting. He was wearing tight-fitting dark jeans and a brown leather jacket, and he looked very much like a normal person as opposed to a history teacher.

'Yeah, but where's Wilde? She can't have stood him up, not with him looking like that!' Flora muttered under her breath, while trying to look inconspicuous. This was hard as Rosie and Daisy were giggling loudly and fluttering their eyelashes in the direction of their unsuspecting teacher. Mr McCabe was looking around anxiously, presumably for Miss Wilde.

'Look, there she is! Ha! I told you, didn't I? I knew she'd turn up. Look, they've seen each other. Shall we go over now or . . .' Rosie was trying to decide when to make her approach, but it had already been decided for her. Flora and Daisy were on their way over to talk to their teachers. Rosie watched from a distance as Mr McCabe's aura changed from green to yellow as

Flora and Daisy approached. Miss Wilde's did the same. They were obviously panicking at the sight of two pupils approaching them. Rosie felt bad. Maybe they should have left them alone. They were entitled to their lives, weren't they? But it did prove one thing: the auras worked. She had worked out about their secret love fest. She had worked out where they would be and now she could tell what they were thinking. She couldn't wait for Flora and Daisy to return and tell her what the teachers said.

After excitedly relaying the story to Rosie throughout all the trailers, Flora and Daisy were loudly shushed by the people in the row behind them. This shut them up long enough to watch the film. As they filed out almost three hours later, Rosie, with evidence of her skills, began to formulate her plan. A grand plan that was to become one of many.

MY SPEECH

Friends, teachers and Heads of Year, lend me your ears . . .

I have a dream, a dream that one day there will be equality for all Year Eight students! That we shall all rise up and create one voice, a voice of unity! A . . . freedom . . .

Maybe Rosie needed to have a think about this

speech-writing thing. It wasn't as easy as she had first thought. Some research was called for. As the following day was a Saturday, Rosie's mum was on the late shift at work. According to her mum, they got most of the nutters in on Saturdays: DDDs – drunk, disorderly and dim is how her mum referred to them. So Rosie had the house to herself, apart from Tess, their neighbour, who 'house-sat' when her mum worked nights. Rosie was adamant that she didn't need a babysitter at her age. Her mum, however, wouldn't let her stay in the house on her own. It was Tess, or staying at Flora or Daisy's. Rosie couldn't stay at either of theirs this weekend for various reasons, so Tess it was.

It wasn't too bad. It could have been worse. Rosie could have been packed off to her dad's every weekend, like lots of people in her year. Rosie hadn't ever experienced the weekend dad thing. She had heard all about it from friends: weekends where you spent all day Saturday trying to have fun, going to MacDonald's, or the cinema, or doing other divorced-family activities, and then spending Sunday waiting to go home to return to normal life.

At least Rosie was spared that; she didn't even know where her dad was. In fact, she didn't even know who he was.

Not knowing her dad, or knowing very much about him, used to upset her. A lot. But now she just got on with it. She didn't have a dad. So what? It was normal; plenty of people didn't know their fathers. She had her mum and her grandparents and that was all she needed – or so she told herself whenever she spent the weekend at her friends' houses and saw what she was missing out on. Rosie's philosophy was you couldn't miss something you had never had. Could you?

At least Tess let her get on with her own thing. She didn't bother Rosie at all, except to make her eat something at some point and maybe watch the TV if anything good was on. Tess tended to favour programmes where people tried to win the public over by singing terrible cover versions of well-known songs. She also liked to sing along with the contestants, so it was more a karaoke session for her than a TV programme. It was best to leave her to it.

As she had the house pretty much to herself, Rosie decided to make the most of her freedom. She went into her mum's study to use the computer. It wasn't really a study. It was the box room, which just about coped with a desk and a chair, if you kept the door open.

She was going to do a Google search on speeches

85

and hopefully borrow someone else's words of wisdom. Next, she would win the election. And finally, win Toby McGregor – with a little help from her aura-reading skills.

While the computer connected to the internet painstakingly slowly, she had a quick nose around her mum's emails. There might be something interesting in there for once. Usually it was just stuff from her mum's friends or nurse's emails and newsletters from the NHS. These were painfully boring. She scanned down the list of mail and her eyes rested on an unfamiliar name – *B. Kelly*.

Rosie moved the mouse over the email and clicked it open.

From: B.Kelly@peacelovers.com
To: MaggieSallis@nhs.co.uk

Maggie,
Hi, how are you? I'll get straight to the point. We need to meet up again. It's the same situation but things have got a little worse. I know I said I wouldn't bother you again, but it's serious this time. Sorry.

Can you email me back with when suits? We're in Birmingham at the moment, which isn't too far . . . Let me know. After that we're back in Ireland, so get in touch soon, please?
Peace.
Bx

Who was B? Who signed their email with 'Peace'? It must be someone from work. It was definitely no one Rosie had ever heard of. If it was someone from work, Rosie might have tuned her mum out while she was telling Rosie about them. She did go on a bit sometimes about work people and it was easier to switch off. This 'B' must be going on about the *work* situation getting worse. But then why would she be in Birmingham if she worked with Rosie's mum here?

'*Same situation*' – what situation? This was very strange. Her mum didn't normally have emails like this. And she didn't have secrets – or did she? She'd definitely been weird lately and had been very shifty on holiday. She could be hiding something. Rosie decided to leave the mystery for now. She needed to research speeches, as the pursuit of Toby McGregor was more interesting than her mum's probably dull private life. Rosie knew she'd get to the bottom of it.

With the help of the auras there would be nothing her mum could hide.

After half an hour of research with 136,000 entries on the web, Rosie was a little bored. She had found some inspiration in the form of several speeches by very famous people. She chose four favourites to use as templates on which to build her winning campaign speech and the speech that would surely win Toby's heart.

All of the speeches she found were interesting in their own way. Rosie knew she should take some inspiration from them but she wanted to do her own thing, too, now she had read them. She would take the end of Queen Elizabeth I's speech about there being *more mighty and wise sitting in this seat, yet you never had, nor shall have, any that will be more careful and loving*.

Obviously she'd have to tone it down a bit. There was also a good bit in a speech by Mark Twain that she wanted to use somehow. He had to know something about life as he wrote the excellent Huckleberry Finn books, which they had read in primary school. The bit about women should appeal to all the females in the audience:

'If all the women in this town had a vote today they

would elect a mayor at the next election, and they would rise in their might and change the awful state of things now existing here.'

Everyone was familiar with the American president John Kennedy's speech. She could change 'Americans' to 'fellow classmates' and change 'country' to 'school':

'And so, my fellow Americans: ask not what your country can do for you – ask what you can do for your country.'

And maybe she could end with the *'I have a dream'* speech from Martin Luther King. This would please Mr McCabe and make sure that he didn't think she was talking rubbish when she came to him the other day, asking for help.

'I have a dream that my four children will one day live in a nation where they will not be judged by the colour of their skin but by the content of their character. I have a dream today.'

Rosie knew that these bits would be OK, but she needed an angle – something different and cool to impress everyone with. This called for a meeting with Flora and Daisy. They decided that next Friday would be a good time to meet up at Rosie's, as her mum was on nights. They might even be able to convince Tess to let them watch a certificate 15 film. You never knew which way Tess would go. Sometimes she was like an adult and other times, more like a mate. Anyway it was worth a try, and at the same time they could write Rosie's and Flora's speeches.

★ Grass Green ✳

They convinced Tess to get a horror film out for them, and Daisy and Rosie were engrossed and clutching their pillows to their chests. Flora had pulled her hooded top over her head and had her hands over her eyes, as if she could block out the fear factor, when she came out with something surprising.

'So I am not running for Captain any more, Rose. You can do it on your own now if you want. Should be easier to win that way, – without me there, too, I mean,' she said, interrupting the screams from the TV.

Both Rosie and Daisy dropped their pillows in shock. Rosie reached for the remote and paused the film.

'*What?* Why? When did you decide this?' Rosie asked, questions falling out of her mouth. She had to admit to being secretly pleased, as it would be easier to do it on her own. But she was puzzled as to Flora's sudden change of heart.

'Well, you know, it's a lot of hard work. I haven't really got the time to write speeches. To be honest with you, I'm not that keen on meeting with teachers to argue about school stuff at lunch when I could be doing better things with . . . well, better things, you know. You don't mind, do you?' Flora said, looking from Rosie to Daisy.

Rosie focused in on Flora and saw that she was indeed telling the truth. Maybe she just couldn't be bothered.

'Nah, I don't mind. I mean, it would have been fun and everything, but you know. I'll be all right on my own. You will still help, though, won't you?' Rosie did need their opinion on her speech even if Flora had lost interest with the whole thing.

'Yeah sure, course we will.' Daisy filled in the silence that had been about to descend on the room. 'We'll be your campaign managers, won't we, Flora?'

Rosie could see that Flora's aura was a shiny healthy green. But there was an uncomfortable atmosphere in the room that had little to do with her fear of the horror film which they had turned back on.

Rosie decided to put this to one side and come back to it when she was feeling more confident and more focused. However, she didn't get a chance to do this as Flora's sudden withdrawal from the Year Captain elections was put firmly into perspective when something much more shocking and out of the blue happened.

The fact that it took until the end of October for Rosie to work it out disturbed her. If it weren't for her new-found aura skills, she wondered whether Daisy would have told them that her parents were splitting up at all. She knew on that first day back to school that Daisy had seemed a little odd when talking about her summer holiday. At the time Rosie had thought she was red in the face with embarrassment. Now she understood auras and knew what she was dealing with, Daisy's red aura made sense. She had been lying to them all along. The holiday had clearly been a nightmare and Daisy had been hiding the fact that her parents were getting divorced.

Flora, as usual, had lots of questions. 'Why didn't you tell us? We could have helped. It's been ages since the summer holidays and you've been keeping it a secret all this time? Why? Why would you do that?' She barely left a space for Daisy to try and answer before she was on to the next thought that had popped into her ever inquisitive mind. 'What about your holiday? The villa? Did you go? Was it a make-or-break holiday, then? When did they tell you? Has your dad had an affair?! Oh, poor you . . .'

Before the tirade of questions could continue, Daisy managed to stop Flora mid-flow and fill in some blanks. As Daisy spoke her aura remained a healthy grassy colour throughout.

'Mum and Dad have been arguing for some time. Nothing huge, just about jobs and futures and stuff, not affairs. Basically, Dad wants to go emigrate to Australia. He has been on about it ever since they went on their honeymoon, years ago now. Mum, however, doesn't. She's just got a promotion and said she couldn't uproot us all at this time in our school lives. Dad said she was just thinking about herself and her job and on and on it went for months. They told us on holiday that Dad is going to Oz anyway, on his own. We are all staying here with Mum.'

Daisy had three brothers and they were all about one or two years apart; Daisy was in Year Eight, Oscar in Year Six, Alfie in Year Ten and Freddie in Year Eleven. Some people said having such a large family must be a nightmare. Rosie thought it was fabulous, and would have loved to have had so many brothers and all be so close in age and get on like Daisy and her family. Well, apart from Daisy's mum and dad, that is.

'We got two days into the holiday,' Daisy went on, 'and Mum threw a glass of wine and a plate of pasta at Dad and told him to "Go and get on with it and tell us, rather than drag this painful charade out any longer" or something like that. I think there was swearing. So he did. He's going to Australia and he is going to retrain as a dive charter! He is going to take divers out to wrecks off the Australian coast and then once they have finished their dive he is going to pick them up and bring them back to shore. Then he is going to go off with some blonde Australian bimbo and have lots of tanned, blond children and forget about us, or so Mum says anyway. She's very angry and so Dad is going this weekend. We normally go camping in Scotland at half-term and rough it, which he loves after the posh summer holiday in the villa. Who is going to put the tent up now? I suppose Alfie or Freddie could do it but it won't be the same . . .' Daisy tailed off.

'Are you going to see your dad again?' Rosie asked quickly. 'I mean, of course you are, but when? Will you and the boys go out to Australia? Are they getting divorced?'

Daisy shrugged her shoulders, burst into tears and mumbled something about visiting next summer, but they were spending Christmas with her mum. It was difficult to tell what she was saying through the snot and elephant-style nose blowing.

Rosie watched Flora confidently put her arms around Daisy, talking to her quietly, giving advice. Rosie had absolutely no idea how Daisy felt or what she would be missing once her dad left. Flora did. Rosie listened to the words of advice Flora gave and found herself lost in her own situation. She found herself thinking, *At least Daisy has a dad, and one who wants to keep in touch and have them visit probably. At least Daisy's dad cares enough to take them on holidays, to spend time with them, to care about them, even if it's going to be from the other side of the world.*

Rosie couldn't speak for the pain she felt in her tummy. She felt sick at the thought of her unkind feelings towards her best friend but she knew that if she opened her mouth she wouldn't be able to say anything nice. Rosie's dad had left before she was even born. Her mum had only ever talked about it once. According to her mum, he turned out to be a bad character and everyone concerned was better off without him. But Daisy's dad was nice; he hadn't had an affair, so she couldn't hate him. He was just following his dream, but this meant leaving poor Daisy and her brothers behind with a very angry wife. What a mess. Who knows? Rosie thought as she shrugged off her dark thoughts. Maybe not having a dad wasn't so bad after all. It was certainly less complicated.

In their efforts to cheer Daisy up, Rosie and Flora took her out on Saturday while her dad packed up his stuff and drove to the airport. He had taken Daisy and her brothers out the night before for a pizza, to say goodbye, and he had given each of them a return ticket to Australia for next summer.

'It wasn't as bad as I thought it would be,' Daisy told her friends. 'I imagined lots of silences – you know what the boys and my dad are like. It's normally me and Mum that do the talking, but the boys were pretty good at trying to cheer everyone up. The food was really nice, too. I had my usual, Hawaiian pizza. We just talked about Australia and how cool it will be to go and visit him there. No one mentioned Mum and what she would be doing. This was the hard bit, but that's the way it is now, I expect – the not mentioning Mum to Dad and vice versa. Weird, hmmm . . .'

Daisy's dad had said that there was email, texting

and the old-fashioned telephone and even letters to keep them going. In the meantime her dad had bought them a digital camera to share, so they could send him photos of them all. It sounded to Rosie like he was really going to miss them.

They were sat in McDonald's drinking strawberry milkshakes as slowly as people with very little spare money could. They entertained each other by making up stories about the passers-by and the people around the restaurant. This normally made them all smile if one of them was feeling down.

'OK, I've got one.' Flora nearly always went first; she just had a great imagination – all the soap-opera watching helped. 'Right, see her over there, the one with the highlights? OK, so, she is called . . . Beth and the bloke next to her is called . . . um . . . Wayne! And they are getting married next week . . . but as Beth gets the Big Macs in, Wayne is chatting to Beth's mum on the phone and is calling the wedding off! He is going to tell her after he eats his Big Mac. But why, I hear you ask? Why is Wayne leaving Beth at this time in their perfect lives?'

Flora was on a roll. Daisy was hooked and beginning to snort with laughter as Flora explained the deeper and darker secret about Wayne. Rosie tuned out. She'd heard Flora's deep, dark secrets about people like Wayne before. Besides, Rosie had slightly more serious matters on her mind, like the elections for Year Captain that were being held after half-term.

She now had her winning speech written, her outfit ready – the candidates were allowed to wear their own clothes. Rosie even had some music to help her out. But what she didn't have was any idea about how to cope with the nerves that were fighting for space in her stomach; nerves about tonight.

Tonight, Saturday night was THE NIGHT. Toby McGregor was coming over to her house, for the evening, for a date! Well, a date was stretching the truth, but he was definitely coming over to talk about the campaign. Admittedly, Rosie had to remind him a few times, but she was still excited, nervous and hyper. She couldn't help treating it very much like a date, sneaking looks at her watch while Flora and Daisy finished the tale of 'Beth and Wayne' and the wedding that was never to be.

Flora and Daisy were fully aware that Rosie was a little more jumpy than usual but they had no idea why. She had mumbled something about nerves about her speech but it didn't ring true. Had they been able

to read auras like Rosie could, they would have seen a
ketchup-coloured stain around Rosie's head and it had
nothing to do with McDonald's sachets.

Red-Amber-Green

Toby seemed very at home in Rosie's house, which was strange as he had never been there before. Her mum was in the lounge, having insisted on being in the house, even if Rosie wasn't on a date. Which, of course, as far as Rosie was concerned, she firmly was, even if Toby didn't know it yet.

Rosie had spent an hour in the bathroom after racing home from McDonald's earlier in the day. She had straightened her hair into severe submission. She had plucked her eyebrows with her new tweezers, then regretted doing so and filled them in with eyeliner pen borrowed from her mum's make-up bag. Rosie then made matters worse by washing the lot off, leaving the top part of her red raw face carefully hidden by her fringe. What lay beneath was not for Toby's eyes.

She had chosen her outfit with great care: old, worn, casual looking jeans with a wide belt, her strappy black top that made her look at least fifteen and her silver dangly earrings. She finished the look off with ten or so bracelets to match, which clanged and clacked very time she lifted her wrist to check the time. She took them off in the end.

Toby, on the other hand, had clearly dressed in the dark in clothes that weren't on speaking terms with an iron. He must have mislaid his comb and lost a fight with a tub of hair wax, resulting in a look that said he'd just fallen out of bed. In short, he looked utterly gorgeous.

They were sat at the kitchen table, with the door to the lounge closed and their music turned up to create an air of privacy. Rosie's mum kept popping in for 'bits and bobs', or to offer Toby nibbles and drinks. Eventually Rosie had slammed the door shut to give her mum the message. Had she never fancied anyone before?

Rosie was trying to pretend they were in the house on their own and that she didn't have a mum who was watching TV loudly in the lounge, while listening out for them. What did she really think they were going to get up to in the kitchen? Or anywhere else for that matter, as things of a romantic nature seemed to be off Toby's agenda and taking on the world of politics and the school was definitely on it.

'Right, let's get down to it, yeah? OK, so, I'm like a skater dude and you are like, you know, everyone's best mate and that. So, if we team up we've got the whole thing down, covered, yeah? Year Eight sorted. Sweet as!'

As the evening progressed, it appeared to Rosie that Toby was living his life as if he were an American, starring in an American film, about an American skating champion who had yet to be discovered. This made Rosie clench her toes. Rosie also started to notice his annoying tendency to fill out sentences with 'like' and 'yeah', while sniffing a lot and pushing his hair into his eyes. This Toby was watered down at school but here in her kitchen he wasn't quite the Toby she had been expecting.

She had only really spoken to him a handful of times; most of her interaction with him had been carried out from a distance, while staring admiringly at him. The American thing seemed even odder. It just didn't quite work for him, but that aside, Rosie was happy to sit and look at his lips and his face as he rambled on incoherently. Maybe if he stopped talking she would start feeling like she did at school. She tried drowning his voice out with the music, hoping to create the desired atmosphere, but her mum wrecked it all by coming in and asking them to turn the music down, so she could watch her programme.

As Rosie felt her over plucked eyebrows burn and tingle she couldn't help but think that this was turning out to be a disappointing evening. Toby's speech was laid out in front of them on the table next to Rosie's. They'd decided to swap and read each other's speeches and then offer suggestions and comments. The idea had been Rosie's; most of the ideas so far had been Rosie's. Toby seemed happy to be led, which wasn't how Rosie had imagined things would be at all.

Rosie read Toby's short, complicated and very strange speech through twice before turning to see if he had finished hers. Toby was very busy, industriously filling his mouth with Pringles, while holding up his fingers each time he put a new crisp into his very crowded looking mouth. It took Rosie a little while to work out what on earth he was doing. As she was wondering how this was going to help their campaign, Toby started coughing and choking. His eyes were filling up with water and turning a rapid red colour. He began flapping his hands madly around his face, stomping his feet in panic on the wood floor.

'MUM!! Quick! Toby's choking!' Rosie knew her mum would know what to do. She came tearing into the kitchen, grabbed Toby around the waist and hoisted him off his chair, pushing into his stomach and huffing. Several bits of Pringles flew out of Toby's mouth with spit and other stuff that Rosie chose not to over-analyse. Toby then started coughing and huffing himself. Rosie's mum passed him a glass of water. She then pushed him down gently into a chair, telling him to take small, slow sips and concentrate on his breathing while she took his pulse. She looked at Rosie as if to say, 'What the hell's going on?' but Rosie just shrugged her shoulders as if to say, 'Nothing to do with me. He's a boy – what do you expect?'

Once Rosie's mum had reassured herself that Toby was not going to come to any more harm, she removed the Pringles and put them safely away in the top cupboard, out of reach. After a bit more fussing she finally left them alone once more. Rosie wasn't sure as to how to proceed after such a dramatic moment, so she waited for Toby to say something.

'Yeah *(cough)*, that was like, weird, but I did get up to twenty, nearly. Fifteen's my all-time record, so, yeah, the speech, cool, Rosie. It rocks. We are gonna, like, totally wipe the floor with Becco and the rest of them . . .'

Rosie didn't hear the end of Toby's theory on her speech and what a great team they make. Her ears had stopped taking in information after hearing the cringy nickname Toby gave Rebecca, 'Becco'. Rosie had no idea that Rebecca was running for Captain for Year Eight, too. This changed *everything*.

Rosie looked at her watch for the millionth time that evening and saw that she had only a few hours to whip Toby's speech into shape. If they had any hope of working together for success against the Princess, they needed a better plan. Despite the Pringles incident and the annoying skater talk, Toby was still the catch of the year looks wise. There was no way she was going to let him swim back into Rebecca's net. The power of the auras was going to come in handy. *Let the battle commence*, she thought.

The dinner hall was filled, almost to the point of bursting, with Year Seven, Eight and Nine, talking, shouting, laughing, screaming, pushing, shoving, wolf whistling, belching and possibly worse. Yet all Rosie could hear was her heartbeat, thudding deafeningly in her chest. Nervous didn't cover it. Nervous didn't even come anywhere close to how she was feeling. She was stood in the wings on the stage, waiting for her name to be called, stomach doing backflips, hands shaking, feet jigging. Rebecca had gone first, of course, giving a wonderfully arrogant speech. Next up was the first candidate for the boys, about to be followed by Toby and then, eventually, Rosie. She gave herself a little shake and tried to concentrate as Toby swaggered over to the mike and cleared his throat.

'S'up, Year Eight? Yeah! All right. So why me, I hear you ask? Well, why not? For anyone who doesn't know me, I am Toby McGregor and I am going to make the best Year Eight Captain, man. And I'll tell you why. Because I rock, and this school needs someone who can make things happen, you know what I mean? *Yeah, you do!* So what we need here are some radical changes, some shaking up of things and some of our freedom given back, dudes. We need to be in charge of who we are and where we want to go. We need to be the masters of our own destiny, yeah! So if that's what you want, then I can give it to you. Vote for me and we will rock this joint!'

Toby high-fived the air, raised his arms up in triumph and bounced off the stage, convinced of his victory. Rosie shuddered; he hadn't kept in any of the changes she'd made. He had stuck to the original waffly speech and it sounded just as bad as it had in her kitchen. Well, that was that. They were ruined.

As she stood bouncing on the spot with nerves, Rosie peered out from behind the curtain, searching the sea of animated faces for Flora and Daisy. They were stood next to each other holding a large banner up between them.

ROSIE ROCKS! ROSIE ROCKS!
ROSIE SALLIS FOR YEAR EIGHT CAPTAIN!
SHE'S NO PRINCESS, SHE'S ONE OF US!

They were waving and screaming, not that Rosie could hear them above the noise. Her name had been called and someone was pushing her on to the stage. She stepped up to the microphone and tapped it, testing it was on. The boy who'd gone for Year Seven had switched it off by accident and did his whole speech by shouting. Rosie was not going to make that mistake or look that stupid. She cleared her throat in what she hoped was a professional manner and began.

'Mark Twain, writer of *Huckleberry Finn*, said, "*If all the women in this town had a vote today they would elect a mayor at the next election, and they would rise in their might and change the awful state of things now existing here.*" I am appealing not just to the women here but to the men as well. I am appealing to you to rise up in our might and change the *awful* state of things at our school.

'I ask you, who is happy to wear a school uniform when we would be more comfortable in our own clothes, able to express ourselves and our personalities?

'Who is happy to be told information about their own school, by their parents, after they and the teachers at the PTA have discussed our futures without consulting us?

'Who is happy to be told that we are not trusted to go into town because we are in Year Eight?

'And where do we spend most of our weekends without coming to harm? In town, of course, behaving ourselves as we would do if we were allowed in school time.

'Who is happy to sit in assemblies, listening to lectures, readings and other talks that mean nothing to us, allowing us no involvement in the start to our school day?

'In the words of one of the greatest presidents of the United States, John Kennedy, *"My fellow classmates: ask not what your school can do for you – ask what you can do for your school."*

'I may not be the most popular person in school; I am not on the hockey team, the netball team or the tennis team. I am not in the school play. I am not a prefect. I am not going to make Head Girl and I am definitely not going to join the cheerleading team, but I am a part of this school. I know most of the year group as I went to primary school with lots of you. I know all the teachers pretty well and am good at most subjects. I rarely get into serious trouble. My mum is on the PTA and finds out all kinds of information before me about school. Like Martin Luther King, I too have a dream, a dream that someone ordinary like me can make a difference to someone ordinary like you.

'To finish my speech, I would like to quote from Queen Elizabeth I, who said that although there may be *"more mighty and wise sitting in this seat, yet you never had nor shall have, any that will be more careful and loving."*

'Just like Queen Elizabeth, the greatest monarch this country has ever known, although there may be wiser and mightier candidates for Year Eight, if I were chosen I would be very careful about our future and our choices, and I would love to be your Captain! Thank you.'

Rosie paused for breath, wishing she had brought a bottle of water with her, and then started to step away from the microphone. She didn't dare to look up at the crowd to try and judge their reaction. She knew her speech was possibly a bit much, a bit too historically based. Perhaps it was even a bit geeky, but it was the only thing she could think of to make herself sound different to all the others. She knew there would be speeches filled with the normal 'vote for me and I will get more chips in the canteen' thing.

It wasn't until she heard the clapping and the screaming, that she raised her eyes. She was surprised when her gaze met with a sea of green aliens, looking like school kids. Somehow she had tuned into seeing people's auras without even being aware of it! Rosie hadn't felt any pins and needles. There hadn't been any blurring of vision. She hadn't suffered the strange underwater sense of hearing, like an untuned radio station noise. She had been concentrating so hard on her speech, she hadn't even been aware that she was using the aura to see what people were thinking. It was green for positive, green for yes, green for good, green for go!

The votes took twenty minutes to be counted and two seconds to be read out. Rosie ignored the Year

Sevens as they were of little interest to her, but when it came to the names of the Year Eight Captains she was ready, holding hands with Flora on one side and Daisy on the other.

'And now to Year Eight. For the boys, our Captain this year is . . . Sam Winters!'

There was a little moment of shock from Year Eight as everyone tried to remember who Sam Winters was, and then wonder why Toby McGregor didn't win. But once they had got over the surprise there was much cheering and shouting and clapping. Sam stepped up to the microphone, shouted, 'Cheers!' down it and stepped away, raising his hand in a modest wave.

Rosie held her breath; it couldn't be, could it? Not Rebecca, not Princess Rebecca. But then she was teamed with Sam, so it must be. Rosie's stomach stopped churning as she let out a quiet sigh and let go of her friend's hands. Her shoulders sank, her body feeling heavy with disappointment as she imagined the conversation with so many people: 'Oh, never mind. Yeah, Rebecca will be great. No, no, I wasn't that bothered really.' All of which would be a lie.

She had so wanted the position. She hadn't minded about Toby not winning as he didn't really deserve it, but that didn't help her case. Toby had lost and now so would she. But the auras of the audience were confusing her. Everyone was green when she'd finished her speech. Maybe she wasn't as good as she thought she was at reading auras. Maybe the whole thing was a load of rubbish after all.

'And with the most votes, the winner for the girls – and it was a close one, ladies – is . . . Rrrrrrrrrrosie Sallis!'

Phew, Alex really dragged that one out. Rosie's stomach began flipping away again with excitement; her mouth broke into an open, wide smile as she stepped up on to the stage and over to the microphone. She shouted out her thanks to everyone who voted, promised them she would do a good job, stuck her thumbs up at Flora and Daisy and then left the stage, brimming over with happiness. Not only had she won, but her aura-reading skills were intact and more than ready to be put to use for some fun at the school disco, her first priority as Year Eight Captain.

✭ Leaf Green ✳

Sam Winters was in Rosie's art class, but other than that she had no idea who he was or where he had come from – certainly not her primary school. He must be new as Rosie knew almost everyone in their year. She would have to find out more about him if they were going to be working together as Year Captains. It was a shame in some ways that Toby hadn't won, Rosie thought, as she half concentrated on the still-life bowl of fruit Miss Brooks had asked them to draw.

Sam Winters was sat opposite Rosie with a pencil in his mouth, humming to himself quite loudly. Rosie tried to pick up the tune he was humming; it sounded very familiar but she couldn't quite work out who or what it was. It was funny, Rosie continued daydreaming, that she and Sam must have sat next to each other almost every week for nearly a whole term, and she had never really seen him before. She hadn't noticed him or spoken to him, which felt strange now.

They were meeting this lunchtime to discuss their plans for the social calendar. Had she simply ignored Sam? Had he tried to talk to her? Rosie was looking at Sam while wondering all these different things and hadn't noticed that he was looking right back at her. Miss Brooks, their art teacher, cleared her throat and interrupted their mutual staring.

'Erm, Rosie, you're dripping water all over your work. Maybe you should move to a table on your own – you might concentrate better.'

Some of the class laughed at this. It was clear she had been sat staring at Sam with her paintbrush hanging from her hand. She had ruined the little bit of work she had done, which to be fair wasn't a work of art by any stretch of the imagination. Art didn't come easily to Rosie, nor did hiding her embarrassment. She picked up her work and shrugged at Sam as if to say she had no idea what Miss Brooks was on about. Sam winked at Rosie and then put his head down and busied himself with the banana he'd been painting. It was troubling him; he just couldn't get the curve right.

'I can't believe *he* just winked at *me*,' Rosie whispered indignantly to Flora, who was sat a few tables away and had been watching the scene with interest that only a best friend can show. Flora and Rosie had been separated in the second art lesson of term. Miss Brooks had quickly realised that they would never achieve anything other than intense chatting if she left them sat next to one another. Luckily for them, Miss Brooks was busy in the store cupboard, tidying the supplies away before lunch. 'Sam Winters! He just winked at me, like we know each other or something!'

'Serious? He winked at you? That's well freaky. Dad's wink and uncles thinking they are being ironic, but Sam Winters? Mate, you have got a weird fellow Captain there.'

Flora's older brother, Matthew, was back from university for Christmas, even though it was only November. Matthew began most sentences with 'Mate', no matter whom he was talking to. It was very difficult not to end up sounding just like him. She was right though; he was a weird fellow Captain to be working with. She'd have to make sure *her* ideas were chosen and not Sam's. Who knew what ideas he would come up with? Winking! Winking at her! What was that all about?

If Rosie thought the winking was odd, things were about to get even more peculiar when they met up at lunchtime. Everything Sam said, Rosie over-analysed.

Using Sam's aura, Rosie checked to see if he was telling the truth and really meant what he said.

'. . . so if we get the teachers on side I can't see why we couldn't have a Christmas Blading and Boarding Day.'

Despite the insanity of his suggestion and his crazy looking lunch, Sam was on green. His aura was a healthy tree-leaf colour. Every time he opened his mouth it seemed he was telling the truth. Rosie scrunched up her eyes to make sure she was seeing his aura clearly.

Since the elections she had been able to simply glance at someone and see their aura almost instantly. She didn't need to work so hard at it any more. Clearly it was a skill that improved with practice. Rosie had been practising a lot, on her mum, her friends, her teachers and people in the supermarket. Anyone and everyone had an aura and she felt she was getting very good at working out what people were secretly thinking. So surely she couldn't be getting it wrong now, with Sam Winters, could she? Sam was still talking, Rosie tuned back in, leaving his aura to hover around his head.

'A Blading Day? I'm sorry, but are you *insane*? There is no way the teachers would agree to us spending all day on blades and boards. There'd be loads of accidents! What about wearing helmets and then getting to lessons on the first and second floors? Then what about those who haven't got any helmets? There'd be casualties; the school wouldn't have insurance. It's madness, absolute madness!'

Sam was smiling, stuffing his revolting ketchup and Marmite sandwiches into his mouth. While Rosie tried not to look at what he was eating, she couldn't help being drawn to the hideous concoction he had made. And why was he smiling at her?

'Why are you smiling at me? And who makes your erm . . . sandwiches?'

Sam continued smiling and chewing, holding his hand up to signal to Rosie to wait, which she did. For some reason Sam, who she barely knew, was seriously annoying her. She really wanted to walk away and go and have her lunch with her friends but they had to get this sorted out.

'Firstly, you sound like a mum going on about insurance and safety. I thought we were supposed to be coming up with stuff that was fun. Secondly, I am allowed to smile if I want, it's a free country. And thirdly, my nan makes my sandwiches for me – wanna bite?'

Rosie scrunched her nose up at Sam's offer of food, sneered at his comment about living in a free country and wondered why his nan made such disgusting sandwiches. Maybe he lived with his nan. She couldn't help checking his aura one more time before looking pointedly at her watch to show Sam she had better things to do and more interesting people to be doing them with. Sam Winters was weird, Rosie decided as she took charge.

'Look, Sam, we've only got ten minutes left before registration and we have to come up with our first social event before Monday. I think we should have a disco. We could do it as a Charity Day thingy and charge money. It could be in the last week of term and we could have it in the dinner hall. I know a DJ, sort of, and it would be loads more fun and much more likely to get the OK from the teachers than roller blades and skateboards.'

Rosie finished her point by folding away the remains of her lunch, tucking her hair neatly behind her ears, smiling and looking pleased with herself all at the same time.

'OK,' Sam replied, ripping open a can of dandelion and burdock, swigging it back in three greedy gulps, crunching it up and putting it in his bag. Before Rosie could comment on his reply she had to ask him something else.

'Why are you putting a can in your bag and not the bin? And what on earth is in it? What's dandelion and burdock?'

Sam smiled again, which in turn annoyed Rosie again as he answered mid-belch. 'I'm taking it home to recycle. My nan recycles all our stuff – everything from potato peelings to cartons of milk. Did you know that even nappies get recycled these days? *Burp!* To answer your other question, dandelion and burdock is a sparkling soft drink infused with natural ingredients and sweetened with fruit juice. To you it would taste a bit like apple juice. It helps to purify the toxins in your system. You should try it – much better for you than that Coke. So a disco it is. Shall we meet up tomorrow to work out all the details? I'll bring you a can. See ya.'

And he got up and walked off, still smiling, leaving Rosie fuming.

The fuming continued at a heated level throughout French that afternoon. Daisy and Rosie had both been moved up to set one and were pretending to translate a short passage about the seaside. In reality, Rosie filled Daisy in on her lunchtime meeting with Sam.

'I mean, how dare he? It was my idea to have a disco and he makes out like he thought of it! Ordering me around, telling me when we should meet and that he'll bring me a can of his weird drink with his weird sandwiches. Why couldn't Toby have won, then at least he would just sit there looking good and let me make all the decisions?'

Rosie barely came up for air before she continued with the next instalment. After checking to see who Mrs Saunders was helping, ensuring it was far away enough that she wouldn't overhear or notice them chatting, Rosie continued informing Daisy about Sam and his strange habits.

'Then he puts his can in his bag like some old bag lady and walks off, still smiling at me. Huh! I mean who is he?'

Rosie couldn't get her head around Sam at all. She had never met a boy like him before and the only colour she could get from him was green. No one had just one colour aura. People's auras changed with their moods and circumstances but Sam's was always green and it was beginning to annoy Rosie. No one could be that honest and positive, could they?

Of course, she couldn't tell Daisy what was really bothering her about Sam and his seemingly innocent and perfect aura. How on earth could she explain all about the auras and Florien's Fates and Fortunes? She would have to tell her about all the things she had worked out using the auras, like Mr McCabe and Miss Wilde's love fest. It would seem too weird now to suddenly confess to this new skill. But the longer she left it the more awkward she felt about keeping a secret from Daisy. Daisy had told her everything about her mum and dad splitting up, her dad moving to Australia and how hideous things were at home. Daisy might wonder if Rosie had worked it out before by looking at her aura.

No, it seemed best to leave it for now. Maybe she'd tell them when they were getting ready for the Christmas disco. They were bound to get ready together. That would be funny – she could make it into a big joke and they could all laugh about it, couldn't they? It was only a few weeks to wait. Rosie watched Mrs Saunders bearing down on their table, coming to check the translation they should have been doing, and her aura was not a happy one.

Saturday night found Rosie home alone once more. No Tess this time as her mum's shift was a short one, so she was trusted to look after herself for a few hours. Rosie would normally relish this time alone. She liked to snoop, eat what she liked, try on her mum's make-up and jewellery and generally do things she wouldn't do if her mum were in the house. But this Saturday she was sat aimlessly in front of the TV with a half-hearted cucumber face pack on, painting her toenails and trying to keep an eye on the time. She was waiting for a phone call. Sam was going to ring. Sam was going to ring her, at home, tonight.

Rosie had no idea where he'd got her phone number. As they left their third disastrous meeting on Friday lunchtime, he had thrown a can of dandelion and burdock at her and shouted out in front of the whole cafeteria that he would ring her on Saturday night to talk about 'things'. He said 'things' in a voice that made everyone around them look up with interest. What things they had to talk about puzzled Rosie. The only thing they had in common was the disco and most of the planning was done.

It must have sounded a lot more interesting to everyone else than it really was.

But why couldn't Sam wait until Monday to talk to her? They had all the details sorted. Now she was nervously waiting for the phone to ring, and when it finally did, Rosie hoped it was Sam so that she could get it over with and relax. It wasn't.

'Hello?' Rosie answered on the fourth ring, not wanting to seem too keen, or that she was sat waiting by the phone, which she was.

'Hiiiiiiiiiiya, my name's Rikki and I am calling from Basics Window Designs. If I can just ask you one question? Good. If you could replace all of the windows in your house, would you?'

It took Rosie a few moments to realise that it wasn't Sam. It wasn't anyone she knew. It was clearly someone either on drugs, someone very hyper, or a coffee drinker. They seemed to be talking complete rubbish. Her mum had told her what to do if a cold caller rang, or anyone trying to sell anything. She put plan 'Mum' into operation.

'Sorreeee, my mummy's not home right now and there are no other adults you can speak to. We live in a new house and have new windows. We don't have any money. Bye-bye.'

Rosie's mum had told her to pretend she was a five-year-old and then put the phone down on them. It seemed to work on the whole, however sometimes, like tonight, they tried ringing straight back! But Rosie was ready.

'MY MUMMY IS NOT IN. GO AWAY OR I

WILL SCREAM AND SCREAM UNTIL I AM SICK! And then I'm ringing the police,' Rosie shouted in her best high-pitched childish voice, to be greeted with the sound of surprised laughter at the other end.

'Well, that's OK. I didn't want to speak to your mummy. I wanted to speak to you, Rosie. But if this is a bad time I can call back when she is in.' It was Sam.

Rosie felt as if she might be sick, while chanting in her head, *Why me? Why me? Why me?*

'Right, Sam, yeah it's just something I do when we have lots of double glazing salesmen trying to ring us up all the time. I didn't know it was you. What do you want?'

In her embarrassment Rosie ended up sounding rude and a bit nasty, which she hadn't meant to. Sam kept catching her off guard and making her feel stupid.

'Right. OK, then. Just ringing to see if you managed to sort the DJ out? You said you knew someone . . .' Sam sounded even more official now. Not exactly cross with her but very 'let's get things sorted'. Now that he was taking that line, Rosie wished he would just chat to her like he did at school. She tried to make things better by starting her own conversation.

'So, I tried that drink you gave me. The burdock stuff. It was really nice, thanks.' Apparently that was the best she could do. She knew she should have written down things to say and put them next to the phone.

This was Daisy's foolproof idea for when boys rang. Not that this happened a lot, but just in case. So that there wouldn't be any awkward silences, Daisy kept a list of possible topics and things to talk about next to the phone. Rosie had laughed at her and said she didn't want to keep Sam on the phone; she wanted to get him off it. But now she wasn't so sure. Now she was listening to a big heavy empty silence and nothing from Sam on the other end of the phone.

'Good.' Sam broke the silence.

'Good, what?' Rosie asked. What was he on about? Good, what? She'd forgotten what they were even talking about.

'Good . . . that you liked the drink I gave you. So is the DJ sorted?' he asked again about the DJ Rosie had promised to line up for the Year Eight end-of-term Christmas disco.

'Yeah, yeah, all done. He'll be there and he's free, too, which is good, isn't it?'

Rosie tried again to get Sam chatting, not entirely

sure why she cared. She should be getting back to staring at Matt Damon.

'Well, it's for a charity, so no DJ fee is the point. See ya at school, then.'

And with that, Sam finished the call.

Rosie listened to the burring noise on the phone and wondered what on earth was the matter with her. For some reason Matt Damon didn't hold her attention any more. She switched off the TV and wandered upstairs to email Daisy and Flora for advice.

To: daisyboo@hawthornhouse.co.uk,
flora.mortimer@yahoo.com
From: Rosieposie@btclick.com

Well, that was the weirdest phone call ever. I messed up by doing my five-year-old thing, thinking it was a salesman when it was Sam. Great start. He was weird – yeah, I know he is weird but he was even more weird than normal. We are meeting on Monday with the rest of the Year Captains and the Head to sort out our events and book out the hall and stuff.

Flora, is your brother still on to DJ? Please,

please, please say yes as I have told Sam I've sorted it and will look really stupid if I haven't, if you know what I mean. Anyway enough about Sam, what about Matt Damon? Did you watch the film? I turned if off in the end. My mum is back in a bit, so I'd better get off the net or she will freak. She's put that parent power lock on the search engines so I can't access any dodgy sites – not that I would want to! She is so paranoid – quick! Delete this message or I will have to self-destruct in case she finds it!

Ooooh, what are we going to wear to the disco? Been so busy sorting it out forgot to sort self out. Need shopping trip, I reckon – next Saturday? Has your mum still got that discount card, Flora? Do you reckon Susannah will do our make-up?

See you on Monday,
Love Rosie x

★ Lime Green ✳

Rosie's mum did not get back from her shift in a few minutes. She did not get back in half an hour. When it got to ten o'clock Rosie began to worry. She had already rung Tess to see if she knew where her mum was, and she didn't. Then she'd rung the hospital, who said Maggie, Rosie's mum, had left over an hour ago and since there was no one else left to ring, she rang her mum, again. Her mobile went to answer phone. Rosie left another message.

'Mum, *where are you*? It's nearly ten o'clock and you were supposed to be home at half eight. Can you ring me to let me know you are OK, please? I'm really worried, this isn't like you!'

Rosie hung up. Her mum wasn't normally late, or if she was she would ring and explain. Rosie didn't want to ring her grandparents as they would worry and there was nothing they could do so many miles away. When the doorbell rang Rosie jumped up to answer it, hitting her knee hard on the coffee table. She knew it couldn't be her mum as she would use her key. It could only be bad news about her mum. Images of policemen and women with their hats in their hands and sad smiles on their faces filled her head as she took a deep breath and opened the front door, expecting the worst.

'Tess! Oh my God, you scared me. I thought you were the police. Do you know where Mum is? Come in.'

Rosie threw her arms around Tess, relieved to see a friendly face.

'Right, let's get the kettle on and make a cup of tea. Your mum's just rung me and asked me to come over and look after you. Yep, yep, she's fine, fine, fine. Don't worry. Chill, Rose.'

Tess moved quickly from fridge to sink to kettle, not quite meeting Rosie's penetrating gaze while she explained why Maggie was so late and, more importantly, where she was at ten o'clock at night.

'She's with a patient, a very ill patient who she couldn't leave and she just forgot the time. She says she's very sorry but she's staying at the hospital tonight until the patient is sorted out. I'll stay here – no, not to babysit, just to keep you company.

Didn't have anything better planned anyway. Fancy watching the telly? I brought some chocolates with me . . .'

Tess tried to steer the conversation away from Maggie and the hospital but Rosie's aura skills were on red radar alert. Tess never lied. There was something funny about all this. She kept bobbing her head when she told Rosie anything and that wasn't right. Rosie decided to ask a few more questions and see what colours she got from Tess. She felt a bit uncomfortable about testing her but then if Tess was telling the truth it would all be OK, wouldn't it?

'Tess, I rang the hospital and they said Mum had left ages ago, when her shift finished. If she was with a patient, wouldn't they know about it?'

Rosie pretended to be stirring the sugar into her tea but kept one eye on Tess, waiting to see what her reaction was.

As Tess answered Rosie's question, Rosie could see that she was telling the truth as she spoke. She continued not to meet Rosie's eyes but her aura was a firm lime green colour and it was very strong. So she couldn't be lying. Her mum must be at the hospital, but why? Who was this patient who was so important – more important than her?

'Your mum's very dedicated. She loves her job and if someone is really ill, or dying even, or haven't got any family, I expect she feels it's hard to get away,' Tess continued. It still didn't explain why she couldn't have told Rosie what was happening. Why she couldn't have rung Rosie to explain all this?

'So why didn't she ring me back? If she's at work she's got her mobile, and she could have used the hospital phones. Why just leave me wondering and worrying?'

It was all very well Tess having all the answers and having spoken to her mum, but it just didn't add up. Tess began to look concerned as Rosie raised her voice and her strong lime green began to look watered down, merging into a lemon yellow of uncertainty.

'I want to talk to her. Where did she ring you from? I'm going to ring her work number and ask to speak to her. If she's there they'll be able to find her, won't they?'

Rosie knew she sounded like a spoilt five-year-old, much like she had sounded only hours earlier on the phone to Sam, but she did want to speak to her mum, very much now. She could see that for some reason Tess was viewing this very simple request as a problem. Her lemon-coloured aura told Rosie very little. Rosie continued to ask questions, hoping that she would find an answer either in colour form or through reading between the lines.

'I still don't get why Mum didn't just ring me and tell me what was going on. How come she rang you? When did she ring you? Did she ring you before I rang you? It's all seems a bit funny. Tess, what's going on?'

Rosie decided subtlety was getting her precisely nowhere. She hoped the straightforward question would give her some straightforward answers.

Tess wandered off into the living room and sat down heavily in an armchair. Rosie turned off the TV and sat opposite Tess, waiting.

'Right, it's pretty easy, Rose. Your mum has got attached to a patient, can't bear to leave them. She lost track of things, forgot to ring you, rang me to ask me to come and look after you and I expect you'll see her in the morning. Now stop fussing and worrying and trying to create a drama out of nothing. Do you want some Fruit and Nut or not?' Tess ripped open the chocolate bar and held it out to Rosie with a look on her face that said, 'Please, no more questions'.

Rosie took a strip of chocolate and watched Tess carefully as she flicked the TV back on and settled back to watch Matt Damon disappearing into the distance.

★ Cherry Red ✳

Sunday turned out to be a freezing cold day with some form of hail-sleet-snow extravaganza flitting out of the sky. Rosie needed a hat, scarf and gloves to accompany her thick coat as she set out to meet Flora and Daisy to go to the cinema. As they were only going to the local one, not the IM, they could walk. However, Rosie was regretting this decision as she shuffled along next to Daisy and they turned into Flora's road to pick her up.

'So what time did your mum get home, then?' Daisy asked, having been given the latest instalment in Rosie's dramatic life.

'About ten this morning, I think. Well, that's when I got up and she was in the kitchen making breakfast and Tess had already gone. She was humming and . . . cooking a full English.' Rosie paused but she didn't need to say any more. Daisy had stayed at Rosie's house enough times to know that Rosie's mum normally considered muesli to be the only food suitable for breakfast. Humming also wasn't an activity that she normally indulged in. Daisy's eyes widened as she realised what this must mean.

'Oh my God, you know what it is, don't you? She's met someone. She's in love. She must have been seeing him last night. Rosie! Your mum's got a boyfriend!'

Rosie looked nonplussed at Daisy's detective skills. 'Well, yeah, I had worked that out, Daisy. It's just I've no idea who he is. I mean staying with some patient in the hospital? It's the lamest excuse. So now I need to find out who he is and where they met and what he's like.'

Daisy burst out laughing as she pushed the sleet out of her face with her sodden glove. 'You think you'll be able to work it out, just like that? If your mum is sneaking around and making stuff up, she's hardly likely to tell you about her new boyfriend, is she? She's probably seeing how things go, and if he's worth it she'll introduce you. Or, maybe she's worried about what you will think, so she's waiting for the right time. That's what I would do, I think. I wonder if my mum will get a boyfriend . . .'

As Daisy chattered on, Rosie realised that she was thinking about using her mum's aura to tell her what was going on and, of course, Daisy had no idea about all of that. No one had, in fact, just Rosie. It seemed like it wasn't only her mum who was keeping secrets, and it didn't feel good, Rosie decided, as they rang Flora's front-door bell.

Their film showing at the cinema was cancelled at the last minute. Due to the bizarre bad weather hardly anyone had turned up and the manager decided it wasn't worth running the show for just seven or so people. Rosie didn't really mind but Flora was very cross. Her mum, being a barrister, had drummed into Flora her rights and how to assert herself. Flora was in full flow when Rosie had a brilliant idea and stopped her.

'Listen, Flora. It doesn't matter. Let's go to the shopping centre instead. Come on, we can see if there's a sale on in Gap. We could get something to eat and then catch the bus home. It beats going home and watching *Songs of Praise*!'

Rosie knew exactly what she wanted to go shopping for. A book. Not just any book, but a book on auras. She had her well-read copy of *Dr Star's Signs of the Times* but that was limited in its information about auras. She wanted something more detailed. Rosie knew she could only go so far herself with making it up and trying things out, but now she needed real help with reading auras properly.

Things were getting more serious at home and Rosie needed to work out what was going on. Her mum had been weird since before the holiday. Maybe she'd had this boyfriend back then. Who knew if it was even her first boyfriend or one of many. Whatever was going on Rosie needed help finding out and this was the only way she could think of as she couldn't just come out with it and ask her mum. Rosie knew she would lie and pretend there was nothing going on, and then she'd be even more secretive and careful and Rosie would never find anything out. The best thing to do was get a book. Then she could learn more about auras. When the time was right and her mum unaware of what she was up to, she would find out exactly who this man was and what he wanted with her mum.

Then there was Sam, too. He and his perfect green aura, which couldn't be right. She was reading him wrongly in some way and so needed help there as well. He couldn't be as honest as he made out and Rosie was determined to catch him out as well. If she was going to have this skill then it made sense to know how to use it properly.

Rosie found herself in the bookshop, on the first floor in the reference section. She had told Flora and Daisy that she wanted to find a Christmas present for her mum, leaving them safely in the fiction section downstairs. The last thing she wanted to do was alert them or have to tell them about being able to read auras. She just wasn't ready for that at the moment. She had enough going on trying to deal with her secretive mum.

There were lots of books on stars, horoscopes, mind-reading, psychics, fortune-telling and, finally, after being disappointed by many promising titles, she found one single book on auras. *Amazing Auras* by Aurelia Andrews seemed to be just what she needed, despite it being a pricey £9.99. Rosie dug deep and told herself it would all be worth it once she had read it cover to cover. She quickly took the book to the counter and managed to pay and get it in a bag before Daisy and Flora came to find her, having tired of looking at the books in the teen section.

'Shall we get something to eat here?' said Flora. 'It's five past three and the last bus leaves at four. It's all we've got time for really and I've got to finish my geography homework anyway.'

Flora, as ever, marshalled them into making a quick decision. They were at the counter, weighing up the merits of carrot cake as opposed to double chocolate fudge cake, when Rosie saw her. It took a minute or two of wondering which TV programme the woman was from before she realised that she wasn't famous. She didn't know this lady from the TV but from somewhere far less expected. The woman standing a few aisles from the coffee-shop part of the bookshop was the fortune-teller from Florien's Fates and Fortunes.

The woman was flicking through the books Rosie had been looking at moments earlier. Rosie decided that she didn't want to see this woman. There was something spooky about her outside of the fortune-telling tent, as if she was out of place and out of time. Rosie felt very uneasy in her presence. Even though she probably wouldn't recognise Rosie, having seen millions of people, Rosie still hid her face behind her hair while she continued to peer at the fortune-teller from a safe distance.

What was the fortune-teller doing here when she should be off travelling around the world, telling fortunes to people who had come to the seaside? Why was she in the middle of town, in the same bookshop as Rosie, on the same day? Rosie shook herself. She was getting paranoid but just to test her conspiracy theory she decided to wander around the bookshop and see if the fortune-teller followed her.

'I'm just going to have one more look for my mum. See if there's anything else she'd want. Just get me a Coke and a Mars bar; I'll give you the money when I get back.' Rosie made sure she sounded really casual. Flora could always tell when she was lying.

'Well, you'd better go to the romance section, then, as your mum's got a new bloke!' Daisy joked as Rosie wandered off.

At first she pretended she was looking at a book on astronomy. Then she walked over to the section on education, pretending to be looking for a study guide while keeping the fortune-teller in her sights. As she was reaching for a guide to *Macbeth*, Rosie felt someone tap her on the shoulder. She jumped and screamed and knocked a pile of guides to Shakespeare over all at once. It was Sam.

'Oh my God! It's you! You? What are you *doing*?' Rosie almost spat at him.

She pushed Sam and his grinning face to one side, searching the bookshop floor for the fortune-teller. All she managed to see was a glimpse of a red cape flying down the stairs at some speed. Rosie knew instinctively this was her. She must have seen Rosie screaming and jumping and ran off. But why?

'Sam, what are you doing, you idiot?' Rosie was furious with Sam, who clearly thought he was rather amusing and ingenious.

'Just saying hi. Are you trying to cheat on your English project?'

Rosie looked down and saw that she was still clutching a copy of *Macbeth Made Easy*. She put it back on the shelf impatiently and stalked off back to Flora and Daisy, not noticing that Sam was following her.

Rosie plonked herself crossly into the seat they had saved for her.

'Can you believe it? You know I was telling you about that Sam and how weird he was on the phone the other night? Well, he's here, in the shop! He just did this tapping me on the shoulder thing. I screamed like banshee and everyone in the shop looked and then I lost sight of, of – oh, he is so annoying! Why did I ever have to be paired with him? Why couldn't I have simple but stunning Toby instead of weirdo Sam? I mean what he's doing in here anyway, stalking me? Hasn't he got a life? Creeping about in bookshops, sneaking up on people . . .'

Rosie stopped to see why Flora and Daisy were raising their eyebrows and clearing their throats dramatically. She turned around to see what they were signalling at and again caught sight of someone storming down the stairs away from her. This time she didn't have to guess who it was. She realised far too late that Sam had overheard everything she'd said about him and Toby. Everything.

☽ ⊙ ★ White ✳

The book wasn't easy to read. It certainly wasn't in the same league as *Macbeth Made Easy*, but Rosie persisted. This was too good an opportunity to miss. Even though she had school the next day, her English project to hand in and Flora's geography homework to copy, Rosie still stayed up as late as her eyes would allow, trying to speed-read *Amazing Auras*. There was a lot of information and theories to take in. Rosie decided to make a list of all the important points as she read, so that she could consult them over the next few weeks of 'Operation Reveal'. She used the back of her English book. As her homework wasn't getting written she might as well put it to good use.

What is an aura?
- An egg-shaped light outlining a person's body.
- A heat haze radiating all around the person, sparkling with light and energy.

- It has every colour imaginable and all colours tell us something about the person's mood.

<u>What is synaesthesia?</u>
- A mysterious condition in which a person's senses combine. The most common kind is colour synaesthesia.
- A person with colour synaesthesia may see colours around people's faces. They may also see blocks of colour in their mind when they look at the names of people they know, or words they recognise.
- Synaesthesia is a condition found in 1 in 2,000 people. It is known to run in families.
- In other types of synaesthesia, people may experience shapes with tastes or smells with sounds.

Then Rosie came across something in the book that made her read it with her mouth wide open and her heart on pause:

<u>Red Overlay</u>
People are not born with a red overlay. It is something that is created over a period of time – a time in which the person has been hurt and has felt a need for protection. Although a red overlay can offer protection, it also can become a terrible burden for the person.

Someone who is carrying a red overlay is suffering intense anger and rage and if the red overlay is not removed from their aura, this colour shield will soon become their prison.

It is impossible for anyone to remove their red overlay as long as they continue to believe that life is not safe or that the world has wronged them. They must let go of the past in order to free themselves and embrace their future.

Rosie knew that this was what her mum had. Even when they had been travelling home from the fair and they both had red auras, her mum's was so much more violent and passionate a colour than hers was. It all made sense. Her mum was still angry at the world. Her mum was still angry at her father for leaving them and angry with her life in general. Until she stopped lying to Rosie she wouldn't be able to get rid of her negative aura and be happy again. Rosie decided to write a summary of what she had learned so far.

Basically . . .
Either there are people who see auras and use these coloured halos or outlines to work out what people are feeling and thinking . . .

Or there are people who have a condition called synaesthesia, which means they may associate colour with certain words or numbers or music.

Then there are the really bad cases, like my mum, with red overlay, who need real help to get on with their lives.

So I see auras because I asked to. Well, I asked to see traffic lights above people's heads so I could work them out, which was never really likely to happen. So seeing auras is the next best thing the fortune-teller could do for me.

I definitely don't have synaesthesia; at least I don't think I do, because I only see colours around people, not words.

So how am I going to use this to work out what Mum is up to?

1. Follow her and see where she goes and what aura she has around her head.
2. Ask her questions about where she's been and who with and look at her aura.
3. Look at her email again and see if there are any clues there.
4. Ask my grandparents if they know what she is up to (could go horribly wrong if they don't know and then ring her and tell her what I've been saying).
5. Quiz Tess again. She is very bad at lying.

6. Get rid of Mum's 'red overlay' aura and help her get on
   with her life.

Rosie paused her list-making as her mum tapped on her door to tell her to turn the light off. Rosie's heart was pounding. That could have been close if her mum had just charged in. Rosie shoved her English book back in her school bag and hid *Amazing Auras* in her drawer under several pairs of thick black school tights. Hmmm, it was all very well her mum pretending everything was normal and telling her to turn her light off as it was a school day tomorrow, but Rosie knew now that her mum was up to something. She felt much better equipped to find out exactly what it was.

As they only had a short amount of time left to finalise all the details about the NSPCC Christmas Charity Disco it was unavoidable for Rosie and Sam not to meet. Indeed, Miss Wilde was insisting upon it. Despite Rosie's best efforts to convince her that all was in hand, she had arranged another lunchtime meeting with Rosie, Sam and herself to ensure that all would go to plan and that there would be no mistakes. As Head of Year, Miss Wilde took herself very seriously, and as Rosie's form tutor of nearly two years, Rosie knew when not to argue with her. Sam was early for once, and sat in the library, doodling on a huge piece of art paper. Rosie crept up behind him and placed her hands over his eyes hoping that some light heartedness would excuse her rant in the bookshop on Sunday.

'Guess who?' she called out.

'Rosie,' Sam replied flatly.

OK, thought Rosie, *I'm not going to be forgiven so easily*. She opened her mouth and tried again, making sure that she was relaxed enough to read his aura, too.

'Whatcha drawing?' Rosie gestured to Sam's piece of paper.

'Well, as you can see, I am designing tickets for the Christmas disco.' Sam stated the obvious in a perfectly polite but 'I'm really annoyed with you at the same time' voice. As ever his aura was a shiny healthy green and it was clear he wasn't lying. He was, in fact, designing some *amazing* tickets for the disco. Rosie was most impressed but tiring of trying to make Sam forgive her for her unkind outburst and less than friendly behaviour in the bookshop. As she didn't know Sam very well she wasn't sure what to try next and was, for once, more than relieved to see Miss

Wilde stride over with her notebook, looking terribly official and important.

'Right, good, you're both here. Sam, how are the ticket designs coming along?'

'Yep, good thanks, miss. I tried out the stuff that Miss Brooks suggested and it looks all right.' Sam smiled and began chatting away to Miss Wilde as if she were his new best friend and someone he liked. *This should be interesting*, thought Rosie as she gently let her eyes relax and tuned into Sam's aura. Annoyingly, it remained the same green colour as it had when she had been trying to cheer Sam up. It would appear that he really did like Miss Wilde and wasn't just being polite. Sam was so annoying. Why was he so nice to Miss Wilde yet so horrible to her but his aura didn't change?

Rosie interrupted the new best friends. 'So, what's left to do then, miss?' Rosie wanted some input into this conversation; she was beginning to feel like a spare part.

'Well, hmmm . . . the DJ? Sam tells me you've hired someone for free. Have they done any events before?'

Now Rosie knew that Flora's brother, Matthew, hadn't really done an event before but she had heard him in his bedroom and he was really good. She decided to tell a little, mini, teeny-weeny, tiny white lie that wouldn't hurt anyone.

'Yeah, loads. He's really good and he's free which is the main thing, isn't it, Sam?' Rosie appealed to Sam to back her up, but he just shrugged and carried on with his designs. *Well, fine*, thought Rosie. *You've had your chance. I've tried to apologise and be nice and you clearly don't want to know, so I give up. I can't work you out anyway. You're too much trouble.*

'Good, good. OK. Well, I'll let you carry on with these great tickets, Sam. If you sort out the printing with Miss Brooks then I'll sort out the distribution with Rosie. That's it, then. The catering is being done by school, lights by the drama department, DJ booked, tickets nearly ready and caretakers are happy to work overtime. So that just leaves advertising. Could you knock up a couple of posters, too, Sam, and then Rosie can put them up around school? I'll make sure it's mentioned in assembly and a note goes in the registers. OK, must go as I'm on lunch duty. Well done, Sam, lovely stuff. Rosie, can you get the register, please?'

And she was flying off through the library, telling Year Nine boys to tuck their shirts in on her way.

Rosie turned back to Sam hoping for a smile, or a funny comment about Miss Wilde, but he was packing up.

'Sam, look, I'm really sorry about what I said in the bookshop on Sunday. I didn't mean it, really. I was just, well, you made me jump and stuff and I was in a bad mood and . . .'

It was no good. Sam was smiling and nodding at her as if to say 'It's OK', but packing up too quickly for Rosie to get any good readings of his aura. He was gone before she could continue trying to read him. Great start to their working relationship as Year Captains! Rosie wondered again why Toby McGregor couldn't have won; life would have been so much easier.

Rosie met up with Flora and Daisy at the gates at the end of the day to walk home. They were deep in conversation about clothes and hair and accessories. Rosie tried to join in, but her heart wasn't in it. There was only so much you could say about the merits of glitter eye shadow over hair mascara. Rosie's thoughts were fully occupied by Sam and how she had made him feel. She didn't need to see his aura to know she had made him feel bad. She tried to explain how she felt to Flora and Daisy, who had noticed how glum Rosie looked.

'What's worse than the fact that I was horrible to him, if you really want to know, is that Sam now knows that I fancy Toby. Well, used to fancy Toby, as I don't any more. I *so* don't, Flora!' Rosie was adamant that she was over Toby. It had only taken the Pringles incident in the kitchen and his terrible speech to show her that looks weren't everything.

'Yeah, yeah, whatever. So if you don't fancy Toby any more, why does it matter that Sam knew you did?' Flora asked.

Good question, thought Rosie. *Why on earth should it matter what Sam thinks?*

'I reckon that you like Sam!' Daisy the detective declared.

'No, no way. I'm serious. That's easy, I really don't. Nope, I've no idea why he is bothering me so much.' Rosie summed up her thoughts on Sam. This time making sure that he wasn't lurking in some bush behind her as she talked about him again. 'I don't even know him, not really. All I do know is that he lives with his nan, eats weird food, drinks stuff that old people drink and is good at art. There's nothing to fancy there.'

'Look, let's change the subject,' said Flora. 'But just to make sure, you don't fancy Toby? You don't fancy Sam? And most importantly you aren't wearing your knee-high boots to the disco? So can I have them?'

Daisy rolled her eyes at Rosie and they carried on their walk home, arguing over Rosie's boots, Daisy's leather jacket, Flora's four-inch heels and other items in their collective wardrobe.

Prism

Schoolwork took a back seat as autumn and its leaves lay all over the floor, ready to be swept up by winter winds and the avalanche of Christmas, which Rosie welcomed. Christmas always provided great distraction from life and the real world. It allowed her to bury herself in pleasant thoughts of presents, festivities, warm fires, chocolates, good telly and seeing lots of people. Of course, this year, above all else, it meant that on the last Friday of December, the day they broke up for the holidays, the NSPCC Christmas Charity Disco would finally arrive. After all the planning, awkward meetings with Sam and Miss Wilde, poster putting-up sessions with half of her tutor group enlisted and the trips to charity shops and any other cheapy clothes outlets, they were ready to face the music and dance.

Flora had invited Rosie and Daisy and a few other girls around to her house to get ready. Even her sister, Susannah, was going to help out and do their make-up, which was a real bonus as she was training to be a beautician. This choice of career annoyed Flora's mum, who strongly believed that Susannah could 'make so much more of herself'. Translated, this meant that she wanted both her girls to follow in her footsteps and be lawyers. Flora had already decided that she wanted to be a criminal investigator after watching several series of the TV show *CSI* (*Crime Scene Investigation*), she just hadn't managed to break the news to her mum yet.

Rosie was so excited about the disco that she had managed to forget about the troubles with Sam and the secret that her mum might be keeping. Although, lately, her mum had been even more predictable than normal: arriving home early, not working so many night shifts, making sure Rosie did all her homework on the night it was set and other annoying Mum stuff. Rosie had begun to think that she might have over-reacted and imagined it all. In fact, the prospect of her mum having some secret life or boyfriend was laughable really. This was her mum, not some woman in a soap opera. For starters, where on earth would she meet anyone when all she did was go to hospital to work and shopping? Rosie knew her mum was much happier watching TV on a Saturday night than going out with some boyfriend as if she were a teenager! Rosie wouldn't mind going out with some boyfriend on a Saturday night herself, especially as she almost was a teenager. It would be ridiculous if her mum had a boyfriend and she didn't. It would be much worse than ridiculous: it would be totally humiliating.

With the promise of dancing away at the disco on Friday night, the last week of term seemed to spin by. Card-making in art class was a welcome relief from the round of DVDs they had been allowed to watch in most lessons. The only drawback to card-making was sharing her table with Sam. He was sitting peacefully, designing an almost professional looking Christmas card which made Rosie's primary school effort pale in comparison. Rosie had given herself a good talking to a few days ago and had resolved not to let Sam get to her. They had met every day last week at school and Sam had been polite, kind and helpful. But he hadn't been friendly or relaxed in the way he had when they first met, before Rosie had upset him. She knew this was all her fault but couldn't see a way to resolve the issue.

Sam had just started humming a slightly off-key Christmas carol when Rosie's brainwave hit her. She could resolve this awkwardness between them and show Sam that Toby McGregor meant nothing to her. Not that it was any of his business anyway, but still, this would sort everything out.

'Sam, I've been thinking, we should go to the disco together! What do you think? I could meet you outside the hall about seven?' Rosie gave Sam her best smile and couldn't help but grin even more when she saw him look delighted with her suggestion.

'OK!'

Short and sweet, but at least he was smiling at her now. Sam moved his chair slightly closer to Rosie's and leant over her work, making a few adjustments with his paintbrush, which changed Rosie's *Blue Peter* efforts into something slightly more cohesive.

'Well, ' said Miss Brooks as she leant over their table, 'it still isn't in Sam's league, Rosie, but the improvement he's made seem to have marked the end of any hostilities between you two. Merry Christmas!'

'What is she on about?' Rosie said, shrugging off Miss Brooks's embarrassing comments once their teacher had turned away.

'Who knows? She's OK, though, isn't she? And she's right, your card does look a bit better. I'm making this one for Nan. I'm giving it to her at midnight mass. We always go together on Christmas Eve. Wanna come?'

Sam was Sam again. Although Rosie hadn't known him for very long, this was the Sam she had been looking for since the bookshop incident, and now he was back she was very relieved – enough to be won over by a simple request.

'OK. I've never been before. We don't go to church. Won't your nan mind?'

'Nah, Nan's really chilled. She'd love you to come – the more the merrier, she'd say. Uh oh, that's the bell. Gotta go. I'm meeting my mate Hallam at break. He's in charge of the lights and we gotta check them for Friday night. Miss, can I leave this here until the end of the day? It needs to dry.'

Sam jumped up, leaving his card on the table, grabbed his bag and ran off in the direction of the hall. Rosie glanced at his card. It was really amazing – he was so talented. It was the kind of card you would happily buy in a shop. Rosie was so relieved they had 'ended their hostilities' as Miss Brooks put it, and Sam seemed happier, too. She wasn't so sure about going to midnight mass with him and his nan, but it would be an experience. It would be a chance to make friends properly.

★ Seeing Red ✽

Flora had the attic room in their three-storey town house, which was good because it meant lots of privacy. It was also huge, and easily slept several people on mattresses on the floor, so Rosie and Daisy were staying the night along with Sadie, Ruth, Kim and Louisa, who were all coming around to get ready, too; they had all been to primary school together. Some of them were down in Susannah's room having their make-up done while the others got dressed. They were all going to gather in the kitchen at half six for punch, which Flora's dad had hinted might be mildly laced in honour of the occasion.

Rosie and Daisy were doing their hair while they waited for their turn to be made up. The noise level increased dramatically as Flora turned up the music once her parents had left the house. They had wisely decided to have a glass of wine and a quiet meal out while the girls got ready. Susannah had been left in charge.

'Right, Rosie you're next. Come and sit here. OK, so fair skin means easy on the make-up as we don't want to turn you into a ghost. I'm just going to put a bit of eyeliner in the corners just to open up your eyes. As they're brown you can get away with a deep purple eye shadow, which will complement your top . . .'

Susannah chattered on in a quiet, relaxing voice as she skilfully made Rosie look at least fifteen in an elegant way. Not in the 'I've fallen into my mother's make-up bag and just slathered on everything' result, which if left to her own devices is how Rosie would have ended up. As Susannah applied lip colour with a brush Rosie drifted off into a daydream, imagining the evening ahead – wondering if the evening she and Sam and Miss Wilde had worked so hard on would all go to plan. As she thought about lights and music and who she might dance with she tuned into the general conversation.

'Can I borrow your lip gloss, Ruth?' Sadie was reaching her hand out for the make-up, adding the finishing touches to her already perfect look. Ruth was trying out her fifth hairstyle on Daisy as she waited patiently for her turn with the make-up master. The music was still pumping out from Flora's room. The radio had been keeping them in the party mood for an hour or so, when someone switched it off to put on a CD. As they did, the conversation filtered down from upstairs.

'Yeah, but she says she doesn't like him any more, that means you can go for it . . .'

Rosie's sense were awoken, and she sat up and began to grin at Daisy, wondering who was being discussed.

'I know, but she did like him for ages and you know what she was like when he went out with Rebec . . .'

Rosie didn't hear the rest of the sentence as the bass kicked in to a new track on the CD, but she felt she'd heard enough. Leaving her seat at make-up central Rosie took Daisy by the arm and led her to the privacy of the bathroom. After shutting the door firmly behind her, she asked her a very simple question.

'Daisy, does Flora fancy Toby McGregor?'

They were stood in front of the mirror. Rosie watched with an air of fascination as Daisy's aura materialised in the mirror, forming a cloak of Christmas red around her carefully put-up hair.

'No, no. Why do you . . . Oh, I don't think they were talking about him and you . . . It could have been anyone really. Shall we go back in?' Daisy asked hopefully.

Even if Rosie hadn't seen the red aura which told her that Daisy was covering for Flora, she still would have known she was being lied to. 'How long has she liked him for?' Rosie asked.

Daisy sighed, looking at the floor. 'Since you wanted to be Year Captain.' This was a really difficult situation for Daisy, as she was caught between her two best friends.

'What? So she lied to me? She said she didn't want him and that she wasn't running for Captain because of him and me. I can't believe her! I knew she was selfish, but this is unbelievable. So . . . what? She's planning to get together with him tonight? At my disco? In front of me?' Rosie was shouting now.

'Well, you did say you didn't fancy him any more. She thought that you would be OK with it now you've got Sam.'

Rosie was too angry to see the sense in what Daisy was saying. She was already thinking about what she was going to say to Flora.

'But I haven't got Sam! We're just friends, I told you both that. Right! I've had it with her.'

Rosie flung open the door and marched up to

Flora's room just as Flora was pulling on Rosie's boots.

'Well, you can take those off for a start! I hear you think you're going to pull Toby tonight? Thanks for telling me! Some friend you are. What were you going to do? Get off with him on the stage in front of everyone?'

Someone had turned the music off and there was a painful silence filling the room. Kim and Louisa, who had been encouraging Flora in her right to Toby moments earlier, edged away from the two best friends, who were both red in the face. They began to inch their way downstairs to join Susannah and the others, who were all holding their breath, wondering what was going to happen next.

How was Flora going to get out of this one? They weren't given the chance to find out. Rosie spun on her very high heels (borrowed from Flora, but she had neatly forgotten this detail in the heat of the moment) and shoved Daisy aside as she stormed dangerously down the attic stairs. She carried on storming until she had slammed the front door behind her. Once out in the cold, without any way of getting to the disco, Rosie knew her only option was going home – to her mum.

✦ Candlelight ✳

Rosie lived near Flora and was very grateful for this geographical fact as she shoved her hands under her armpits in an effort to keep them warm. Her mum would wonder what on earth was going on and ask lots of questions and be furious that she hadn't rung her to be collected. She would say things about 'catching her death of cold' and 'if she wanted to be ill for Christmas she was going the right way about it' and that 'anything could have happened to her on the way home'. Rosie knew she was right and had considered ringing her mum, but she had already charged halfway home before she even thought about where she was going and what she was doing.

She didn't often lose her temper like this. She was surprised at herself and the scene she had created, and on tonight of all nights. It was going to be ruined now, really horrible and uncomfortable, and she was supposed to stay at Flora's. Well, there was no way that was happening now. Rosie wasn't sure whether she was even going to go to the disco.

She couldn't believe how quickly things had gone so wrong. The walk home had given her time to think about what she was going to say to her mum. As she turned the corner into her road she saw a car pulling away from her house, beeping as it drove off into the cold night. Rosie wondered who had been round. She saw her mum draw the curtains in the living room as she put her key in the door.

'Bri— oh? Hello, love, what are you . . . ? Oh, Rosie, what on earth's the matter? Oh, come on, come here, love.'

Rosie's mum wrapped her arms around her daughter and guided her to the living-room sofa as Rosie sobbed out what had gone on at Flora's house.

'Well, you did say that you didn't like him any more. I thought you said he was an idiot? I know that's not the point, but you can see why she might think it was OK.'

Rosie's mum was saying everything that Daisy had and it was not what Rosie wanted to hear. She wanted to hear her mum say what a bad friend Flora was and poor Rosie. She pulled away from her mum and blew her nose.

'Well, yeah, but still, Mum, she shouldn't have told

everyone that's what she was going to do. She should have told me first, then I wouldn't have minded.' Rosie sniffed in a disgruntled manner.

'Did you expect her to ask your permission? It's not as if you ever went out, is it? You weren't his girl-friend, were you? Well then, come on – let's get your face washed and I'll drop you off at school.'

Wash her face? Did she not realise how long it had taken to achieve this look? Rosie stood up to look in the mirror and burst out laughing. Her mum was right; she did need to wash her face. She looked like a panda with mascara smudged all around her eyes. Susannah would be horrified.

As Rosie washed her face in the bathroom and applied more mascara, not with the skill and care of Flora's sister but reasonably well, she wondered what she would say to Flora when she turned up. She wondered what the girls had all said to each other after she'd stormed off. Maybe they'd all hate her; maybe they were all talking about her and what a drama queen she was.

Rosie's mum was waiting in the car, having warmed it up. Rosie got in, with her own shoes on now, having taken Flora's off.

'Your gran and grandpa will be up tomorrow, ready

for Christmas Day on Sunday. Have you got all their presents? Do you want to come shopping with me tomorrow?' Her mum was trying to take Rosie's mind off things as they drove to school.

'No, I've got them stuff. I'll probably be tired after tonight. Can you pick me up too? I'm not going to stay at Flora's, so can you ring her mum and say sorry for me, please?

Rosie squirmed with embarrassment in her seat at having to ask her mum to do her dirty work for her. She was beginning to feel that she might have over-reacted. If she could just get to the disco and find Flora and sort it all out, she knew she'd feel much better.

'OK, don't worry about it. I'm sure it'll all be sorted out once you get there.'

Rosie's mum turned on the radio, admittedly to Radio Three, but it was better than nothing.

'So who was at ours when I got home?' Rosie began making conversation.

'What?' Rosie's mum jumped and almost stalled the car as she changed gears badly.

'When I came round the corner there was a car leaving our house. I just wondered who it was.'

Rosie looked closely at her mum, who was shoving

her hair behind her ears and making frantic hand gestures as she spoke.

'Oh, no one. It must have been someone parked outside ours but seeing someone else. OK, so what time do you want me to pick you up?'

Rosie could see without any effort that her mum's aura was a fiery red, and then the obvious sudden change of subject made it a certainty. Her mum was lying again. There *had been* someone at their house, someone who had just left in a car, and her mum was lying about it for some reason. Enough was enough. Rosie resolved that once she had sorted things out with Flora and Christmas was over, she and her mum were going to have a conversation. There would be no lying and no way out for either of them. This was getting beyond a joke.

☽ ★ Disco Lights ✱

The lights were working brilliantly, the music sounded seriously good and the room was packed. On the left side were most of the girls and on the right, most of the boys. Where was Flora? Rosie wondered as her eyes searched the crowd.

'Guess who?'

A voice came from over her shoulder, and hands went over her eyes at the same time.

'Sam!' Rosie shouted, pleased to hear a familiar voice, and she turned around to see his smiling face. Sam handed her a red box, wrapped tightly with a bow on top.

'This is for you. Merry Christmas.'

Sam was beaming and he looked like he had made an effort with his clothes and hair. Rosie felt a mess next to him, hoping he couldn't see that she had been crying.

'Oh, I didn't get you anything,' she apologised as she looked around for somewhere to store her present.

'No worries. I didn't do it for that. Are you gonna open it now?' Sam grinned and gestured to the present.

'No, um, no. I'll save it for Christmas Day. I'll just put it in my locker for now with my coat.'

They began walking up the hallway towards their lockers for Rosie to put her present and things away. As they walked, Sam chatted away about Christmas and the disco.

'The DJ you got is slammin'. Where did you find him? He's been laying down some tracks that would blow your mind. Oh, and I asked my nan about, you know, midnight mass and that. She said to get your mum to drop you off at ours and then we'll walk down together rather than you turn up on your own at the church. Should be all right, some singing and mince pies – might even get some mulled wine out of it.'

Sam chattered away, telling Rosie all about his nan and her Christmas customs. Rosie was listening half-heartedly when she saw Flora walking down the hallway towards them. Flora was coming from the direction of the girls' loos with Kim and Louisa at her side. They were laughing and talking and generally having a great time, until Flora spotted Rosie. Rosie's stomach turned over. She dug her nails in the palm of her hand and tried to smile at Flora, who looked surprised to see her.

'Hi, sorry about earlier. I totally overreacted. Can we make up?' Rosie smiled and shrugged her shoulders at Flora in apology ,waiting for a response.

'Yeah, so shall we go back in, then? There's nothing of interest out here.' Flora linked arms with Kim and Louisa, sneered at Rosie and Sam, and walked past them with her nose in the air, as if Rosie didn't exist.

'Uh, oh, girl stuff. What went down there?' Sam turned back from watching Flora strutting down the hall to be met with a tearful Rosie. He put his arm around her and guided her outside, away from prying eyes and the gossip machine. They walked like that until they reached one of the benches outside the canteen. As they sat down Sam passed Rosie his hankie. It was clean and folded and ironed. She blew her nose with embarrassment and wiped away once more at her runny mascara.

'Want to talk about it?' Sam began, sensing Rosie needed to tell someone.

'Not really.'

Rosie wasn't overly keen to reveal to Sam her feelings for Toby McGregor, despite him having overheard her declaring them in the bookshop a few weekends ago.

'Well, it looks like you have rattled her cage. Not sure what you've done but maybe you should leave her alone, for tonight anyway. Come on, let's go in and see if any of the boys have ventured out of the holding pen and are being brave enough to talk to the girls. Maybe we should set them a good example? Wanna dance?'

Sam jumped up and started doing a very bad impression of what he clearly thought was beautiful ballroom dancing. Rosie burst out laughing, relieved to have stopped crying. She got out her little compact mirror and sighed as she caught her reflection. Hardly the look she was going for, but it would have to do. She couldn't sit outside crying all night, could she?

As they walked on to the dance floor Rosie kept her eyes down. She didn't want to know if Flora was in there or not. Matthew, Flora's brother, who was DJing for the night had just put on some decent music in an attempt to get more people on the floor. Sam held out his hand to Rosie and twirled her around and took over the dance floor. Rosie felt a bit odd holding his hand, but at least he was just messing around, doing silly dancing like he had done outside.

As they spun around, completely out of beat with the music, Rosie started to feel less tense. Sam was grinning away at her, chatting, telling jokes, entertaining her, while making a total fool of himself by dancing very badly. Rosie had stopped worrying about where Flora and her friends were and had a quick look around the room for Daisy. As she searched the girls' area she felt someone behind bang into her on the floor. Rosie turned around to see who it was: Flora and Toby, wrapped around one another and kissing for all they were worth. Flora managed to break away from Toby's lips for a second to raise her eyebrows at Rosie and grin in triumph, just as the music stopped and the track changed.

Rosie stood in the middle of the dance floor, feeling as if all eyes were on her. The silence extended uncomfortably as the amateur DJ struggled to adjust the volume. A slow dance started and Flora turned her back on Rosie as she moved even closer to Toby, wrapping her arms around his neck and placing his hand on her waist. Rosie couldn't see anyone's faces as the lights the drama department had set up were excessively bright, but she could feel everyone waiting to see what she would do. It was clearly common knowledge now that she had had a thing for Toby, that she and Flora had had a fight and that Flora was now challenging her.

Sam had stopped fooling around and was looking at Rosie to see what she would do, too. Rosie wasn't sure, but she knew she had to do something, so she did.

★ Murky Waters ✳

Rosie woke up on Christmas Eve morning with none of her usual anticipation. She was severely lacking in excitement about her grandparents' imminent arrival. She was sorely missing the usual fizzy feelings in her stomach at the thought of Christmas beginning. This year was different. This year she rolled over in bed and pulled the duvet around her ears, blocking out the sounds of the carols her mum was pumping out from downstairs. Rosie hoped the duvet would block out a whole lot more than the music but the Christmas carols seemed to be taunting her, cruelly reminding her of the night before.

Last night was in competition for one of the worst nights of her life. It was even competing with the night she tried to run away when she was six. She had attempted to leave on her roller blades and got as far as the end of the road, fell over, split her lip and had to be brought home by Mrs Fox, the scariest old lady on the street, with a big mole above her lip with hairs poking out of it. Rosie shuddered at the memory.

Despite Mrs Fox and her mole, last night won hands down. To make matters worse there was no one to blame for her behaviour but herself. Rosie groaned as she remembered the moment leading up to 'The Disaster' as she was beginning to call it. She cringed with embarrassment as she recalled the hurt look on Sam's face, the shocked then amused look on Flora's face and the captivated looks on most of Year Eight's faces as she made a spectacle of them all, especially herself.

When she saw Flora kissing Toby it wasn't that she felt anything for Toby, it could have been anyone she was kissing. It was more that Flora was only doing it to annoy Rosie and to make her feel small; to make her see that Flora could have anyone and anything she wanted and Rosie was powerless to stop her. Flora was supposed to be one of her best friends, but Rosie had overstepped the mark with her overreaction and Flora was paying her back for making a scene and ruining her sleepover. Rosie realised all this in one moment on the dance floor. It was this realisation that drove her to turn away from Flora, pull Sam closer to her and lean in and kiss him, much in the way Flora was kissing Toby.

What Rosie hadn't thought through was Sam's reaction to this. At first he barely moved his lips, as if he couldn't move for shock, then slowly and very gently he kissed her back. This wasn't what Rosie was expecting and she pulled away from Sam. Still caught up in her anger with Flora, she had made the mistake of staring at Flora with a look of triumph that said, 'See? I can get anyone and do anything I want to – you're not the only one.' It was this look that Sam was a witness to. It was this look that disgusted Sam and made him realise what Rosie was up to, what the kiss meant to her: nothing at all. He saw that she was just using him to get back at Flora. Sam waited for Rosie to turn back to him, dropped her hand and walked away from Rosie as fast as he could.

'Why me? Why me? Why me?' Rosie groaned aloud into her duvet. She knew the answer; it was just that she didn't want to face up it. If only she hadn't been so wrapped up in Flora and Toby and her mum and the secrets and reading auras. If only she hadn't invested so much time and energy into worrying about Sam's aura not being genuine, she would have seen what was in front of her all along. Something that needed no colours or special powers to reveal itself.

Sam *liked* her.

He had done all along and she had blown it, lost his friendship and more. Rosie knew without looking in the mirror for her own aura that she liked Sam back, but it was too late.

'Come on, sleepyhead. Are you coming downstairs to help me? I need to get the baking out of the way before Gran and Grandpa get here. Rosieeeeeeeee!'

Rosie's mum was in a wonderful mood. She had worked Christmas Day and Christmas Eve last year, so it was her turn to have them off this year and someone else was working her shift in A & E. Rosie knew her mum wasn't going to let her mope in bed all day. Even though she had no idea what had gone on last night, she knew Rosie needed distractions. Rosie dragged herself out of bed, pulled her dressing gown around her and flumped grumpily down the stairs.

The kitchen smelled wonderful. The air was full of a warm, musky sweetness. The window was open to let out some of the heat, as her mum's hair was curling round her face with the humidity. Rosie's mum was taking something out of the oven. She placed the oven tray carefully on the breadboard and turned around to look at Rosie.

'Goodness me, do you feel as bad as you look? Didn't you sleep at all last night?'

She pushed Rosie down into a chair and plonked tea and toast in front of her on the table. Rosie reluctantly buttered her toast and reached for the jam.

'Not really, no.'

Rosie wasn't in the mood for chat, or baking, or her mum, or Christmas. She was in the mood to mope, to moan and to worry about last night and Sam.

'Well, they'll be here in a few hours. I suggest you eat that, jump in the shower and get a wriggle on.'

Rosie almost preferred her mum when she was stressing about work and school and shifts. She ate her toast half-heartedly while stomach-turning scenes played in her head of the disco and her public humiliation.

After Sam had walked away from her, head down, not looking back, Rosie had been left on the dance floor with Flora and Toby. Even Flora looked sorry for her. No one laughed; the silence was excruciating. There was nothing Rosie could do other than leave.

She went to her locker to get her coat, hoping no one would follow her to see if she was all right – they didn't. She didn't even look for Sam. She knew he wouldn't wait around, that he would have gone home to his nan's. When she opened her locker she saw Sam's present sat on top of her coat, in its shiny red paper with a big red bow. She vaguely remembered leaving it in her mum's car last night.

What had she done? Poor Sam. She knew she had to go and open the present, even though she didn't deserve it. A shower and getting dressed would have to wait.

'I'm just going to get something I left in the car last night,' Rosie told her mum as she closed the front door, moving quickly to avoid her mum insisting she get dressed first.

Rosie sat in her mum's car with the present on her lap. For some reason she was nervous about opening it. She couldn't guess what Sam might have bought her. She wondered when he bought it and where and did he ask anyone for advice and did he hope she might have got him something? Rosie's mind was crowded with questions as she slowly pulled the shiny red wrapping paper off.

Inside was a small navy box with tiny gold lettering on the top. It looked like a jeweller's box. Rosie gasped, worried that he might have brought her a ring, or something expensive from a jeweller's shop. She felt guilty again for the way she had behaved, poor Sam. He had gone to such an effort for her and all she had done was use him in return. He must hate her. Rosie looked up to check her mum hadn't followed her out; there was no one around. Rosie didn't want anyone to see, she wanted complete privacy.

She lifted the lid of the box and saw that it was filled with gold tissue paper. She took out the first layer to reveal a thread-thin silver chain. She picked it out and lay it on the palm of her hand. Glistening at the centre was a tiny silver letter – the letter 'R'.

Tears plopped into her hand, making the necklace wobble and blur in her vision. It wasn't diamonds, pearls, rubies, emeralds or sapphires. It wasn't a huge chunky gold necklace but the sweetest, most precious and delicate thing she had ever been given. In fact she had never been bought anything by a boy before and to buy something so dainty and thoughtful surprised Rosie. Who knew that Sam would choose such a lovely gift, with such taste and kindness and care? And now she didn't deserve it.

Rosie shoved the red wrapping paper in the glove compartment, put the necklace back in the box and put it in her dressing-gown pocket. She didn't want her mum asking any questions when she went back in and she definitely didn't want her to see she had been crying again. It was all she seemed to do at the moment. Rosie slammed the front door behind her and ran up the stairs, shouting, 'I'm going in the shower.' She heard her mum mumble some form of reply.

She turned the water on full blast, drowning out voices, thoughts and feelings as she let the water drum repetitively on to her head.

Tinsel

Rosie was feeling about five years old. Her grandparents, who were normally fairly cool, had gone into Christmas overdrive and forgotten that she was a teenager – well, almost – and had bought her a selection box. Rosie knew from the look on her mum's face that to make any comment about it would be very wrong. She said thank you and mumbled something about still being full from lunch and put it in the cupboard.

If only there were someone to share this all with. Christmas Eve on your own, or at least being the only child at Christmas, was horrible. Rosie knew that Flora and Daisy would be arguing with their brothers and sisters. They would be having fun, playing games and watching films together, moaning about doing the washing-up and going out on their bikes, but she was on her own. She felt even more alone than normal as she wasn't speaking to Flora. Daisy probably didn't want to be friends any more either, and not even Sam would want know her now. She was completely alone.

Her mum tried hard enough and her grandparents did their best, but it wasn't right; there was someone or something missing. Rosie didn't know if it was what had happened at the disco or if it was 'the dad thing' that was affecting her. She only ever felt like this at Christmas.

It would take quite a large family occasion, such as Christmas, to get her wondering where her dad was. She would work through the painful process in her mind, asking herself if she thought he was alive, picturing what he was like, what food he liked, music, films and other tastes. Then, finally, her worst fear would creep up on her, lodging in her mind until she had convinced herself that he had another family. A new wife, lovely children, a nice house, probably a dog, too – well why not? It was what every other family seemed to have, except her, and Christmas just made it all worse. There was someone missing.

Every time she asked her mum, all she would say was that he wasn't a very nice man and that he was selfish and ran off, leaving her pregnant with Rosie. She had to admit, he didn't sound like someone you would want to get to know. She knew her mum

185

wouldn't lie to her about that, so Rosie had accepted it over the years. She had asked her gran about it one Christmas, when her mum and grandpa had gone for their after-lunch walk. Her gran had told her briefly and clearly exactly the same thing her mum had and that it was best not to bring it up as she didn't want to upset her mum, did she? Not at Christmas, surely?

Rosie didn't want to upset her mum, not this year and not any year, but she was beginning to resent being treated like a child who was always kept in the dark. It was weird that her gran had said the exact same thing as her mum, not a slightly different version of events, but word for word. Her gran hadn't even met her dad as far as she knew, so how could she know what had really happened? It was as if they had all got together and worked out what to tell her, coming up with the same story.

Rosie shook herself and got on with the job she had been sent in the kitchen to do – tea-making. She was getting carried away with conspiracy theories and her overactive imagination. She knew she was just looking around for a topic to take her away from the real issue: falling out with Flora again, the disaster with Sam, the beautiful necklace and what to do about the whole thing.

The necklace! The wrapping paper was still in her mum's car. She had to get it out before her mum and grandpa went out. They always drove to Whistley Woods for their Christmas Eve walk. They were probably thinking of leaving about now – well, after their cup of tea anyway. Rosie had to get the wrapping paper out before they got in. She didn't want them asking her embarrassing questions about Sam. She could just imagine her grandpa teasing her about having a boyfriend.

Rosie made the tea quickly and without care and took it through.

'Here you go, Grandpa, Gran, Mum. There's sugar in the pot. I'm just nipping outside for a minute – feel full, and want some fresh air,' Rosie gabbled, and was out of the front door, snatching up her mum's car keys before anyone could question her. She could hear her mum muttering about 'teenage hormones' to her grandparents.

Rosie threw herself into the passenger seat and rooted around for the shiny red paper her present for Sam had come in. She looked under the seat, around the back, in the footwell and finally remembered she had shoved it in the glove compartment. She flipped it open and reached in, pulling the red paper out. A whole lot of other rubbish came with it. Car-parking tickets, Tesco receipts, a small bottle of water and a letter. Rosie was about to shove them all back in when she glanced at the handwriting on the envelope. It looked unfamiliar and the postmark was Ireland, which was weird because they didn't know anyone in Ireland. It was dated from a few weeks ago. Rosie took the letter out of the torn envelope and began reading.

Maggie,

Hi, how are you? Sorry to disturb you but I just wanted to know how F was. I'm not on the internet here, so I thought I'd just drop you a quick line as you didn't want me phoning the house. I know you've a lot on your plate at the moment with Rosie and Christmas and trying to juggle it all, but I think what you are doing for him is wonderful.

He really needs someone like you taking care of him. He's been like this for years – always pretending he's OK and that it's old age or life on the road. But I knew it was something more, which is why I brought him to you. I knew you'd be able to convince him. He still talks about you, you know – you and Rosie. He's ever so grateful for the photos, even though he won't say it, stubborn fool.

I hope the operation went well. I'm sure he's recovering

sensibly under your care. Have you thought any more about his request? I know it's a lot to ask but I think if time is running out it only seems fair. I know you've got a lot to think about here but remember you might only get this chance. Think about it and I'll see you when he's discharged.

    Peace,

    Bx

Who *was* this B? And who was F? Why was Mum involved in looking after someone? Why did he ask about them and talk about them? What was going on here? Rosie forgot all about the red shiny paper from Sam and the Tesco receipts that were now all over the floor. She managed to shove the letter back in the glove compartment and get out of the car. She locked the car, opened the front door and went upstairs to her room without even thinking, moving as if she were on auto pilot.

'Rosie, we're off to the woods for our walk. Are you coming?' her mum shouted up. Rosie ignored her. 'Rosie! Are you coming? Come on, even Gran's coming this year! It looks like snow. *Rosie?*'

Her mum sounded a bit cross; she didn't like Rosie to be grumpy in front of Gran and Grandpa. She had a thing about manners and she didn't want them thinking that Rosie was rude or not well brought up. She'd always been paranoid about them thinking she was a bad mother – as if they did! Anyone could see she was a good mum but she did go over the top sometimes. Rosie thought she had better reply.

'No. No, thank you.' She couldn't manage any more. She heard her mum and grandparents chattering away as they got in the car. Rosie breathed a sigh of relief as they drove off. Now she could think.

★ Holly Berry Red ✳

Rosie ran to her mum's study as soon as she saw the car turn out of their road. With a bit of luck they would be gone for at least an hour, an hour and a half. Her grandparents were keen outdoor types and were used to doing what they called a 'good walk', so they should be some time. They had to walk a lot slower now Treacle, their dog, was getting on. That should give her plenty of time for what she needed to do.

Rosie waited impatiently for her mum's computer to come on. She knew what she was going to do was wrong but what could she do? Her mum had left her with no choice. It might be something and nothing, but this was the only way to find out. There were too many questions, too many names running around in her head, too many bits of the picture that needed joining up. As she waited for the internet to connect Rosie went and got out the piece of paper she had kept in her top drawer since the end of the summer holidays. On it were the words of the fortune-teller;

the words that had made little sense to her until now. Rosie reread her notes. She had written them when she had got back to her grandparents' house, wanting to remember every word the fortune-teller had said.

Fortune-teller stuff:
The picture will eventually reveal all. It will open my eyes. To help me she will let me see in colour, help me to build up a jigsaw, fill in the missing pieces to complete the picture.

That's exactly how it felt – as if her life were a picture with missing pieces, a jigsaw to be completed, and it was her mum that held the missing information back from her. Even her grandparents seemed to know more than she did about her own life. *The picture will reveal all* – but how?

She had looked at it at least a million times and it told her nothing other than that he was a tall man, with dark hair and a crooked smile, and he had lots of freckles spattered all over his proud nose. He wore tatty jeans and a T-shirt that had something written on it. It was hard to tell as the picture was an old-fashioned one – a Polaroid, her mum called it; it was torn and had faded over time.

What could this picture reveal to her – this photo of a man, the man she thought might be her dad?

Rosie looked up from her piece of paper and saw that the computer was connected to the internet. She clicked on her mum's email icon and then looked in the inbox. There was nothing there that Rosie thought looked suspicious; nothing from a person called B. She scanned through her mum's sent mail – nothing there either. Rosie sighed; this was no good at all. As she was about to log off she clicked on the deleted messages box before she knew what she was doing and that's when she found it.

From: B.Kelly@peacelovers.com
To: MaggieSallis@nhs.co.uk

Maggie,
Hi, how are you? I know when I came round last night that I said I'd give you time to think, but it's getting too late. You need to talk to him – properly. I went to see him today and I think he's worse. He said you're not in until after Christmas. I thought you were going to keep an eye on him. You know what he's like. He won't listen to me,

and he says he's going to discharge himself if you won't agree to what he's asked. I'm going in on Boxing Day – can you meet me there? We need to talk about the situation. I know you don't want me to come to the house again, so can we meet at the hospital?

Peace,

Bx

Things were not exactly falling into place but points and facts were bouncing around in her head. Some slotted in easily to form part of a picture, but others were great big gaping holes missing essential information.

Rosie made a list of what she knew so far, hoping the simple facts written down might form a better picture.

1. B and Mum send letters and emails.
2. Mum deleted this email.
3. Mum hid the letter from 'B' in her car.
4. Mum and 'B' are looking after someone at Mum's hospital.
5. He seems to know about me and wants to talk to me.
6. Mum has some kind of decision to make about this person.

7. Mum lied about 'B' coming to our house when I ran away from Flora's.
8. Mum might go to the hospital on Boxing Day.

Still to find out:
Who is 'F' and what has he got to do with Mum and me?
Why is Mum lying to me?

Rosie reread the list she had made, reread the latest email from 'B' and reread the fortune-teller's information. She had some of the picture but not all of it. Rosie shut the computer down and sat staring at the blank screen, trying to fit together the bits and bobs she knew. Her thoughts were disturbed when the phone rang. Rosie jumped up guiltily from her mum's chair and ran across the hall to answer it in her mum's bedroom.

'Hello?' Rosie answered, still feeling that she might be caught out.

'Oh, hello, can I speak to Rosie – Rosie Sallis, please?' the voice at the other end asked.

'This is Rosie,' Rosie answered hesitantly.

'Hello, this is Sam's nan, Betty. I thought I'd just give you a quick ring to make sure you know what time we are meeting tonight,' she chatted away.

'*Tonight?*' Rosie had no idea what Sam's nan was on about, how she got her number and why she was ringing her. People's nans didn't ring you. She couldn't ever imagine her gran ringing one of her friends, let alone a boy.

'Christmas Eve, midnight mass. Sam did tell you what time, didn't he, love?'

Sam's nan carried on chatting as if she had known Rosie all her life.

'Um, I, well, I think he said to come to yours at nine but I'm not sure I should still come . . .' Rosie ran out of ideas. She didn't know what to say to this complete stranger. Sam had obviously not told her what Rosie had done on Friday night at the disco. How was she going to get out of this one? There was no way she could go to Sam's house or go to midnight mass with him and his nan. No way. She would have to say no; get out of it somehow.

'Good, so we'll see you at nine and then I'll drop you home after the service. Make sure you bring your scarf and gloves – it looks like snow. Imagine that, a white Christmas! See you later, then, love.'

'Bye . . .' Rosie murmured into the receiver as she heard it click and burr at the other end. Well, there was no arguing with that. She'd have to go. Why on earth didn't she say she was ill? Or that her grand-parents were here? Or that her mum was ill, that her dog was ill, but she didn't have a dog and, oh, it didn't matter! She was going to have to see Sam and a lot sooner than she thought.

☽ ★ Mulled Wine ✳

What seemed like hundreds of candles lit up St Saviour's Church, twinkling away against the backdrop of the tall stained-glass windows, which had been polished ready for the service. Rosie counted all the colours she could. She was amazed at the array of shades and hues of the beautiful artwork and the wonderful story each window told. For a moment, she almost forgot about Sam – all that remained unsaid between them – and his nan, who was insisting Rosie call her Betty. Betty was acting as if Rosie were the nicest friend Sam had ever brought home.

When her mum had dropped her off at Sam's house earlier in the evening, she had stood at the door waiting, wondering what reception she would get from Sam. As she heard someone coming to answer the door, Rosie wished she had been here before. Not only was she worried about Sam and the kiss at the disco and how things would be between them, but she was also nervous in a normal way about going to someone else's house, especially a boy's house.

Betty answered the door, sweeping Rosie into the room, waving her mum off and shutting the door against the cold. Sam came bounding down the stairs and charged into the room. When he saw Rosie he stopped right in his tracks and almost toppled over.

'I thought you said a surprise, Nan! What's *she* doing here?'

He sounded really cross and was looking at his nan in disbelief. The way he said 'she' made Rosie wince. She realised that Sam hadn't invited her at all. He had no idea that she was coming. He must have thought that after what happened at the disco Rosie would stay away and now she firmly wished she had.

'Sam, that's no way to speak about your guest. Take Rosie's coat and hat and gloves and put the kettle on, at once, too!'

Betty was not interested in Sam sulking and ordered him around, keeping him busy while she took Rosie into the sitting room and sat her in front of a real fire.

'Oh, I love real fires. We've only got a gas one at home but I've always wanted a real one. Mum says they are too messy, too much fiddling around with paper and coal . . .' Rosie stopped, realising that she was babbling. She often did when nervous, but Betty could see that she meant what she said about the fire.

'Everyone loves a fire, especially at Christmas. Can't beat it, can you, Rosie? Now will you have scones or mince pies, love? I'm not so fond of mince pies myself, but I make them especially for Sam. He's very fond of them, you know, and mulled wine when it's on offer. Have one of each, sweetheart.'

Rosie was offered several plates all at the same time with cakes and pastries on. All were slightly mis-shapen and home-made, smelling wonderfully spicy and sweet. Rosie did as she was told and took one of each. The cold night air had kick-started her appetite and she always ate when nervous as it gave her some-thing to do.

Sam came into the sitting room with a tray laden with a teapot, tea strainers, tea cups, saucers and small plates. His nan clearly did things properly. The tea cups were like the ones her gran had, pale china with tiny roses all over them and tiny handles. When she was little, Rosie had thought they were made just for her. Betty smiled encouragingly at Rosie, as if to say, 'Don't mind Sam.' So Rosie didn't.

They spent a few hours in front of the fire, talking and eating, and Rosie and Sam slowly made eye contact. At one point Betty left the room 'to get something' and Rosie panicked, thinking that Sam would ask her what on earth she was playing at on Friday night. She worried that there would be an uncomfortable silence, but Sam seemed to be acting normal once he had got over the shock of her arrival. They talked about everything other than the disco – mainly about grandparents and Christmas. Rosie wanted to ask where his parents were but didn't want to risk upsetting Sam, or make him feel uncomfortable that she already had.

When Betty came back, she was dressed for the outside and bossed them about, insisting they wrap up warm as they were walking to church. Betty lived in a tiny cottage around the corner from St Saviour's and informed them that the brisk walk would do them 'the power of good'.

The walk to church was almost magical; the air was crisp and cold but they were all prepared for it. Everyone's curtains were open to show off their Christmas trees and decorations, so they didn't feel bad about having a peek inside people's windows. Each room showed a familiar scene: families sat on their sofas, watching telly together; some people were still having dinner, entertaining guests, and there were still a few children up, not ready to give in and go to bed just yet.

Several other people were walking to church, too; they would make their annual appearance there in honour of Christmas.

Betty placed herself between Sam and Rosie and linked arms with them. She claimed she needed the support. Betty was one of those people who made you feel at home straightaway, as if you had always known her. She reminded Rosie of Sam in some ways, but in others they were very different – Betty was a lot bossier. Even though he was chatting to her and making jokes and being his normal self, Rosie couldn't help but wonder if things would ever be the same. Could they could go back to being friends again when his nan wasn't around?

The sermon was like most sermons, long and incredibly boring. Rosie's attention drifted off in parts and returned to looking at the beautifully coloured windows. When she looked across at Sam she saw he was doing the same. They caught each other's eyes and giggled, sharing in their conspiracy. Betty, who had been listening to the sermon intently, gave them both a pointed look.

As Rosie leant back in her pew she reached for her

necklace, the silver necklace that Sam had bought her for Christmas. She hadn't been sure about whether she should wear it or not, but was glad she did now as she twiddled the letter 'R' around, completely unaware that Sam was still looking across. On seeing Rosie wearing his necklace his face broke into a delighted smile. He leant over and whispered in Rosie's ear. 'What are you doing on Boxing Day?'

'Nothing much,' Rosie replied. 'Mum's going into hospital – she'll probably be gone all day. Why?'

'Just wondered if you fancied meeting up?' Sam said with a grin.

'Sure, um . . . why don't you come over to mine and we can watch some DVDs and eat leftovers and stuff?' Rosie suggested, trying not to sound too excited. Was this a date? she thought. It didn't sound like one – more like two friends hanging out – but she had a butterfly feeling in her tummy. She was just so happy Sam had been able to forgive her; that they could start again.

'OK, shall I come over about lunchtime, then? I'll bring some stuff with me from –' Sam's plans were interrupted by a terse 'shush' from Betty as everyone rose to their feet to sing the next carol. This put an end to any elaborations on their Boxing Day plans.

Rosie smiled at Sam and received a cheeky wink in return.

The singing of carols was the best part. Rosie loved Christmas but wasn't really interested in the religious side. She wasn't against it, but it wasn't something she felt she could give her full attention to. She had enjoyed the nativity play the local nursery put on. The story they told was one she had heard and loved when younger, but now she just wasn't so sure what she thought about the whole God, Jesus and the Holy Spirit thing. But she still loved Christmas and was glad to be there with Sam and his nan and a packed church full of smiling people all happily gathered together, even if it was just for one night.

Betty drove Rosie home, dropping her off outside her house, and waited until she had opened the front door before waving and driving off. Rosie had a quick cup of tea and a chat with her grandpa, who had stayed up for her, filling him in on the service before they said goodnight and went off to bed. Rosie's mum and gran had given up trying to stay awake just after midnight apparently. Rosie was glad it was just her and Grandpa. She wasn't sure how to act around her mum at the moment.

The car journey over to Sam's nan's house had been

quiet and awkward. They hadn't said very much to one another. Nothing of importance anyway, which felt odd as Rosie knew there was so very much that they should be saying to one another. Her mum had been a bit moody about the whole thing, about her going off on Christmas Eve and leaving the family. Rosie had almost wished her mum would say she wasn't allowed to go, but she seemed to give in at the last moment and insisted on driving Rosie there. Maybe she felt uncomfortable around Rosie too?

The service with Sam and his nan had come just at the right time. She didn't want to spend the evening with her mum, watching everything she said, reading her aura to see if she was lying. Wondering whether her grandparents knew what was going on as well would have made for a very uncomfortable evening.

Rosie knew she needed some time alone with her book on auras to prepare herself for Boxing Day. If her mum was going to be sneaking around in hospitals, visiting secret people, then Rosie wanted to be ready for her. She was going to catch her out and work out what was going on and why it was such a big deal. She just had to get Christmas Day and her grandparents out of the way first. She didn't want to make a scene in front of them or ruin their Christmas. Besides, where on earth would she start in all of this mess? Rosie needed a plan.

Gold

Christmas Day came and went like most Christmas Days before it. There were presents, there was the tree, television specials of soaps and sitcoms, crackers with tacky little presents and awful jokes. As usual there was far too much turkey, followed by the heavy, rich Christmas pudding with heavy, rich cream. It was all perfect, apart from one thing.

Rosie spent the whole day testing her mum, watching her and trying out different theories. She wanted to give her mum the chance to own up to whatever it was that she was hiding, but she didn't. Rosie provided several conversations and appropriate topics for her to explain herself, to reveal the big mystery and tell the truth, but nothing came of it. Either her mum pretended to miss the point, stuck to neutral topics or left the room to check on the dinner. It wasn't until her grandparents went that Rosie realised her feelings and endeavours to get her mum to confess hadn't gone unnoticed. She was in trouble, big trouble.

'What on earth was the matter with you today? You've barely said a word to me and when you did none of it made any sense. Have I upset you?' Rosie's mum was drying up the dishes in an aggressive manner, as if her life depended on it. 'Even Grandma and Grandpa asked what's wrong with you! Going off to your room all the time, asking odd questions, sulking and then disappearing on Christmas Eve to go to church with some boy you've only just met! Then you spend the whole day snapping at me and giving me funny looks. After all the effort I went to to get Christmas just right . . . What *is* the matter with you?'

Rosie's mum flung the tea towel down on the worktop and stopped her manic activity to turn around to face Rosie.

Rosie had been waiting since Christmas Eve for her mum to ask her what the matter was, so she could say, 'Ha! Why don't *you* tell *me*, Mum?' But now the chance presented itself she had no idea what to say.

'Dunno,' Rosie mumbled into the sink. They were washing and drying up together and there was a lot more to do, but her mum pulled Rosie's hands quite sharply out of the sink and forcefully guided her to the table, gesturing for her to sit down. Rosie was surprised by her mum's behaviour but knew what was coming next.

'*You* are going to sit there and tell me what's wrong. Then we are going to have a long talk about your behaviour of late, *young lady*.'

Arrrrggggghhhh! There was nothing, nothing, nothing on earth worse than being called 'young lady' by your mum. Rosie cringed as soon as she heard it and knew that she couldn't tell her mum about reading people's auras. She couldn't tell her mum about the letter and emails she had found, and worse of all, she couldn't tell her mum about Sam and how she felt about him. People who said 'young lady' would never understand or believe half of what Rosie had whizzing around in her muddled head. She would have to make something up. She dug her nails into the palm of her hands as she thought about what to say.

'Is this all about Flora and Daisy and the fall out you had? *Yes?* Then why on earth don't you just ring them up and ask them to come around tomorrow night? I'll even pay for you to get some DVDs and pizza and nibbles and they can stay over and you can all make up. Hmmm? Rosey Posey? Is that what this is all about?'

She wasn't angry any more; instead she was tucking

Rosie's hair behind her ears and stroking her cheek absent-mindedly and calling her the name no one else did in the softest of tones. Rosie was almost ready to forget the whole thing. She began to lean her head into her mum's soft hand and close her eyes, ready to wish it all away, but her mum carried on talking and changed all of that.

'I've got to do a shift anyway. I'll be in the hospital most of the day – can't have Christmas Day off and expect Boxing Day off, too, can I? So some company would be good for you and Tess is always just next door. I'll ring Flora and Daisy's mums and sort it all out. You finish the washing-up and then you can watch telly. OK?' After kissing the top of Rosie's head she left the room to go and use the phone. She didn't even wait for Rosie to answer. As far as her mum was concerned, this was their little chat all done and dusted. Super-mum had solved all Rosie's problems and now she was going to ring her friend's mums and sort out tomorrow evening for her, like she was a kid . . . Rosie's thoughts stopped dead.

Tomorrow night was Boxing Day night. Her mum had just said she was working a shift at the hospital! She couldn't have Flora and Daisy here. She needed to follow her mum to hospital and find out what was going on. It was her only chance. This was all too convenient, her mum keeping her occupied on the night that she was secretly meeting this 'B' person at hospital. She had to stop her and quickly.

Rosie rushed to the door but saw her mum in the hall, chatting away on the phone to either Flora or Daisy's mum. As she chatted she gave Rosie the thumbs-up, as if to say, 'I've sorted it all out. Don't worry – you and your little friends can make up tomorrow night and I can sneak off and see my new boyfriend and keep it all from you.' Well, there was no way on earth that was happening. Rosie had to come up with a plan to somehow get out of the house without Flora or Daisy noticing. Bearing in mind neither of them was speaking to her, it should be an interesting evening. It would certainly beat watching more Christmas specials on TV.

Ivy

'Mmmnnn . . . Hello?'

Rosie was still half asleep as she answered the phone the following morning, rubbing sleep out of her eyes. She waited for the person on the other end of the line to say something.

'Hello!' Rosie shouted this time, starting to get annoyed. They got so many marketing phone calls. Her mum kept threatening to go ex-directory and hide their phone number but never got round to it. Rosie was just about to hang up when she heard a voice.

'Oh, sorry, Rosie love, I hadn't turned my hearing aid up. Ah, I can hear you now. It's Gran, love. I need to speak to your mum – just a quick chat. Is she there?'

Rosie grinned, trying not to laugh at her gran; she had a bit of trouble with her hearing aid. Rosie shouted for her mum to come to the phone.

'Rosie, don't bellow like that, you sound like a fishwife!'

Rosie's mum took the phone from Rosie and swished her away from the phone with her hand.

'Morning to you too, Mum!' Rosie replied. She decided she might as well get up now she was awake and anyway, she was on Mum red alert today. She pretended to make breakfast in the kitchen while eavesdropping as best she could.

'No, no. It's all right. Yes, but I've got to, haven't I? Or I'll look like the one in the wrong. No, not yet. I will, I will tell her, but in my own time. No, definitely not, no. Thanks anyway, though. I know you mean well, but it's best if you leave it to me, Mum. It's my mess to sort out.'

Oooh, well, all of that sounded intriguing, but without hearing the other side of the call it was very difficult to work out what it could be about. Her gran only ever rang on Sundays, every week without fail, at three o'clock on the dot. Today was Boxing Day, it was first thing in the morning, her gran hadn't even asked how Rosie was or what she was up to, which she always did, and so this was definitely not a normal call.

Rosie wished she could read minds properly. Being able to see people's auras was useful to a certain extent but it had its limits. Her mum's aura was a bright green when Rosie poked her head around the corner to look. Unfortunately, her mum must have sensed her presence because she ended the call rather quickly. Rosie rushed back into the kitchen and shoved some bread in the toaster.

'So! What are you up to today, then?' Rosie's mum began as she bustled about, making tea and putting jam on the table. 'You've got a few hours to kill until Flora and Rosie come around. They'll be here about lunchtime and I –'

'Lunch? Lunchtime? But I thought you said they were coming round for tonight?' Rosie started to feel panicked. She wasn't ready to see either of them yet and certainly not so soon. This was not going to plan. 'They can't come round at lunchtime as . . . well . . . I've already made plans, with Sam actually. You should have asked me first, Mum,' Rosie mumbled under her breath, knowing she was sounding ungrateful.

'It'll be fine, don't worry. You'll say sorry and they'll say sorry and you can sort everything out. I'm sure whatever plans you've made can keep. Sam won't mind waiting. You could see him tomorrow, couldn't you?'

Rosie's mum was so preoccupied that she put the

teabag and spoon in the bin together and the toast in the fridge.

'Mum! What are you doing? You've put the toast in the fridge. What's up with you? Was it something Gran said?' Rosie asked carefully as she turned around from the fridge to face her. Her mum was sat at the table with her back to Rosie. Rosie didn't need to see her face when her mum answered to know that she was lying, as her aura was a flaming red one.

'Gran? No, no. Just chatting about her, um, hearing aids – not working again! Right, I'll grab some breakfast later. I've got to go into town before work. I need to do a bit of shopping, so I'll get lunch there and then go on to work. Tess is staying the night too; no, don't argue, Rosie, that's what's happening. Right, I'll be gone in an hour and then I'll see you tomorrow morning. I'll ring you around teatime to check you are OK. There's money in the jar for the DVDs and I've put pizzas in the freezer. You can get some popcorn and chocolate at the video shop. OK. My mobile will be on, so if you need me don't call reception at work. They get so busy around this time of year what with all the idiots overdoing the food and drink, then they wonder why they are feeling ill and . . .' Rosie's mum carried on her conversation as she left the kitchen to go and get dressed, leaving Rosie without a shadow of a doubt in her mind that her mum was lying to her, again.

There were two problems she had to contend with before working out what all the lies were about. Problem number one was Flora and Daisy, who would be arriving for lunch in a little while. Problem number two was that Sam would be there, too.

Surprisingly, Sam being there when Flora and Daisy turned up was the best thing possible. Sam took over; he was the joker, the entertainer and the reconciliation official. He had brought a picnic made by his nan, containing an assortment of odd sandwiches and wonderful cakes and weird sounding drinks. Flora had brought several boxes of chocolates and Daisy had brought all the new CDs her dad had sent her from Australia as a Christmas present. At first it was really awkward, there was no getting around it, but Sam took Flora and Daisy's coats as if he were the butler, making sure that the silence that met them all as they stood in Rosie's hallway didn't last long.

'This way, please, ladies. Do follow me . . .'

Sam led them to the dining room, where he and Rosie had laid the table with all the goodies her mum had bought, all the food from his nan and a few crackers left over from Christmas. Rosie hugged both Flora and Daisy, said sorry again and then poured them tall glasses of dandelion and burdock.

Sam clinked the side of his glass with a knife. 'Please raise your glasses, ladies, in a toast. To friendship, with all its highs and lows. Cheers! Oh yeah, and Merry Christmas 'n' that.' Sam ended the formalities by gulping down his whole glass and belching heartily.

All three girls rolled their eyes at one another and smiled properly for the first time. Over the plates of food and glasses of strange concoctions they sorted out their differences. With a few mumbled apologies and a lot of help from Sam and bad-taste jokes from the Christmas crackers, all seemed mended.

'So are you and Toby an item, then? Not that it's any of my business and I don't mind or anything . . .' Rosie tried to sound less confrontational. She didn't want either Flora or, more importantly, Sam to think that she still fancied Toby. Daisy looked a bit nervous and Sam waited to see what Flora's answer would be as he filled his mouth full of food.

'Nah. He's all right, but not much going on in the conversation department. I might just see him casually. He's gorgeous, though, isn't he? Such a shame!'

They all burst out laughing, feeling mean for laughing at Toby but at the same time happy to use him as common ground to pull them back together as friends.

'Talking of items, what gives about you two, then?' Flora whispered as Sam went back into the kitchen to get kitchen roll to mop up Daisy's spilt drink. Rosie paused before she answered, trying to think through what she could say. She wished she could smile and say 'yes' they were an item. She would love to be able to tell her friends that she and Sam were going out, seeing each other, boyfriend and girlfriend, but the answer was no. Nothing was going on and Rosie felt really sad for a moment, like she'd lost something and knew that she wouldn't be able to find it again. Before she could answer, Sam came back in and the question was forgotten for the time being.

With Sam there the three friends were on best behaviour. No one wanted to sound petty or immature, so they silently agreed to forget the disco, the disaster and never mention the whole fiasco again. With Sam there they became their best selves; they were funnier than normal, cleverer, kinder and more relaxed. Even though Sam wasn't Toby and wasn't someone they fancied, both Daisy and Flora wanted to impress him, wanted him to like them and wanted everyone to get on. Sam had that effect on people, Rosie realised. And for her part, she very much wanted to impress him, too, but without him knowing it.

They watched a few films, they ate a lot of food and talked a lot about school, people they knew, Christmas, families, presents, the ever increasing burden of parents and the embarrassment of siblings – well, Flora and Daisy did, and Rosie and Sam, being only children, listened avidly. When Tess turned up at eight o'clock they weren't even aware of the time. She informed them that she would be in the living room, watching decent stuff on the telly, and they could do what they wanted. Sam took Tess's arrival as his cue to depart.

'I leave you fair ladies in the company of the kindly neighbour and bid you all a goodnight.' He picked up his coat and put his boots on, smiled at Rosie, waved goodbye to everyone else and stepped out into the night to walk home.

As soon as the front door slammed shut Flora and Daisy marched Rosie up to her room, sat down on her bed and ordered her to 'spill'. Part of Rosie was desperate to talk about Sam and how she felt about him, but at the same time she didn't want to say it out loud and didn't really know how to put it into words anyway. So Rosie ended up telling them something else entirely. She chose to confide in them something she wished she had months ago, right at the beginning when she first realised what was happening, instead of keeping one of the biggest and most difficult secrets of her life.

'You know when I came back from my gran's and I was a bit ill, on the first day of school?' Rosie began, taking a deep breath and letting it all tumble out. 'Do you remember? Then a few weeks later we fell out over the Year Captain elections and everything was a bit funny between us all? Well, when I was on holiday my mum and I went to a fair –'

'You? You and your mum? You went to a fair?' Flora couldn't help but interrupt. 'Both of you? But she's never let you go to one before, not even once in your life? Why now?'

'Exactly, but that's not the point. There's loads more . . . I went and saw a fortune-teller and she asked me what I wanted to know. I said I'd like to read people's minds, know what they were thinking about.

Do you remember my theory, that if we all had traffic lights above our heads then at least people would know what we were thinking and it would give us all an idea about who fancied us, if we were right or wrong and if our parents were lying to us? Anyway, it turned out that she couldn't do exactly that, but she did give me a gift. She sort of granted me my wish.'

'So you are telling us that you see traffic lights above people's heads?' Daisy asked with a smirk on her face, not believing what Rosie was telling them. 'Come on, Rosie, there's no way!'

'No, it's not as simple as that. What she did was let me see people's auras. You know everyone has an aura – a colour in the shape of a halo around their head? Well, each colour represents a mood, or a feeling. So if someone's lying they normally have a reddish aura and green if they are being honest,' Rosie explained. This sounded so silly now she was saying it out loud, but it was the truth and the truth was long overdue.

'So you can see a colour around me now? What colour am I, then?' Flora said, testing Rosie.

'Well, you are a greenish colour; you're not lying about anything and are feeling positive,' Rosie answered, sighing at all the interruptions. She still

221

had so much more to tell them and realised that time was running out. It was nine o'clock already and she had to get to the hospital somehow. She really needed their help and in order to help they needed to know the full story. If only they would shut up and listen.

'OK, OK, do me. Do my aura,' said Daisy, wanting to join in, too.

'Hang on; let's see if this *really* works. Ask Daisy a question and then you can tell from her aura if she's telling the truth or not,' Flora suggested, still not convinced.

'OK, um ... Daisy, did you have a good Christmas?' Rosie began, struggling to think of something to ask her.

'No, that's really boring. Let's ask something interesting. OK, I've got it ... Daisy, do you fancy anyone at the moment?' Flora asked with a glint of mischief in her eye.

Daisy blinked a few times and looked Rosie in the eye when she replied, 'No.'

Rosie couldn't help but smile.

'What? What?' Flora desperately wanted to know what Rosie could see that she couldn't.

'OK, well, Daisy has a tangerine aura. This means that she does fancy someone, but maybe she's not totally sure about it yet. Or perhaps she's torn between two boys?'

Daisy burst out laughing at this. Rosie had got it exactly right.

'OK, you got me. I'm stuck between two potentials but not sure which one is *the one*, if you know what I mean,' Daisy replied and smiled at Rosie, not minding being caught out.

'Who? You never said! What are their names . . . ?'

Flora began what Rosie knew would be a long inquisition. She had to stop it and get them back on track.

'Shut up! Sorry, but listen. I've got more to tell you and you keep going on about boys. This is much more serious. OK, so I've got this aura thingy and I can read people. You know when I knew all about Miss Wilde and Mr McCabe? Well, it was cos I read their auras. Remember the audience at the debate? You fancying Toby, Flora? And you and your mum and dad splitting up, Daisy? When you came back from Florida I knew you were lying about something, but I didn't know what. So it does work and you believe me, yeah? It's important that you do before I tell you the rest . . .'

Rosie paused to check that Flora didn't need to test

223

her any more. They both nodded at Rosie and encouraged her to tell them the rest of the story.

'On holiday Mum was weird – yeah, I know, but even more weird and stressy than normal. When we got back and I worked out that I had the ability to see and read auras, I thought I'd try it on her. I found out that she is lying to me, all the time, about something or other. Then I found a letter in her car from some-one called B, from Ireland. I'd already read an email to Mum from her, and then after I found the letter there was another email in Mum's trash tray . . .' Rosie was struggling to tell them everything all in one go. She stopped and pulled out the emails she had printed out and got out her notes she had scribbled down after reading the letter, and then pulled out her lists of facts. They poured over the information and tried to work out what was going on.

'You said your mum is at the hospital now? Well, let's get over there and find her and see this "F" per-son for ourselves. Maybe if you just turn up it will fall into place,' Flora suggested, excited at the prospect of something different and unusual to liven up their lives now that the excitement about Christmas had worn off.

'Yeah, but what about Tess? We can hardly sneak

out without her noticing, can we?' Daisy cautioned Flora, who was up and ready to run out of the front door. Flora sat back down. They sat in silence for a few minutes, stumped with the problem of the kindly neighbour who was sitting in the living room, next to the front door, laughing her head off at the Christmas sitcoms.

★ Cranberry Sauce ✳

The great escape wasn't as great as they had hoped, but it was an escape of some sort. Flora's brother and sister had been roped in, as the girls knew they would get nowhere without someone who could drive. Flora had been chosen as the speaker and Daisy and Rosie looked on uninterestedly as she explained to Tess where they were going and why.

'Yeah, my mum just phoned and said that she would prefer it if we all stayed at my house as both she and my dad are there. They've got my relations coming around tomorrow and want me there bright and early. My brother is coming to pick us all up. My mum said she owes Rosie's mum a favour and will be happy to have us and stuff, so that frees up your evening. She's rung Rosie's mum and left a message on her mobile. Bet you're relieved that you can go back to your own home and do your own thing, not stuck with three teenage girls all night!' Flora meant to make a joke of it and sound like she was doing Tess a favour, but

Rosie noticed that Tess looked really disappointed and a little bit hurt. She had popcorn in one hand and the DVDs they'd chosen in another.

'Oh, cool, thanks, Tess. We'll take those with us and watch them later.' Daisy smiled as she took the films from Tess and put them in her bag. Rosie felt awful and tried to smile at Tess, too.

'Oh, right. Well, it looks like you've sorted it all out and your mum's OK with this, is she, Rose?' Tess didn't seem sure that this was the right thing to do.

'Yeah, yeah, she knows Flora's mum really well. They are on the PTA together. Least it gives her a bit of peace and quiet when she comes home in the morning. 'Spect I'll see you tomorrow anyway. Think Mum is having a drinks thing for the neighbours. Are you going to lock up, Tess? I'll take my key with me.'

While Tess locked up, Rosie ran back upstairs to her room and grabbed the photo from *Dr Star's Signs of the Times*. She wasn't entirely sure why, but it was the only bit of the puzzle she hadn't told Flora and Daisy about – and in many ways, the most important bit. It felt right to shove it in her jeans' pocket.

Flora's brother was waiting in the car and Rosie knew his patience would only last so long. Tess gathered up her things slowly and took ages locking up the house and leaving lights on to con any potential burglars into thinking someone was in. So Rosie let her get on with it and gave her a quick hug before jumping into Matthew's car with Flora and Daisy.

'Right, you want dropping at the hospital, do you? Then what?' he asked as they turned out of Rosie's road and headed for the hospital. They all looked at each other; they hadn't got that far in their plan. They'd got Susannah in place to answer the phone and pretend to be Flora's mum, just in case Tess or Rosie's mum rang. Flora's parents were at a party with friends and wouldn't know what they were up to, or so they hoped. They thought they had all areas covered – except what to do when they got to the hospital.

'Shall we try and find this "F" person first, or your mum? Or shall we just try and follow her or look for the "B" person? Will either of these people know what you look like – you know, will they know who you are?' Flora as ever was full of questions. Rosie had very few answers and Daisy looked on in sympathy.

Rosie had thought that Daisy's parents splitting up was the worst that could happen, but at least they had been honest in the end and told her and her brothers what was happening. Rosie, however, was totally in the dark. What next?

It was a good job Matthew was there to take charge. 'OK, this is what I think you should do. Find out what room this "F" dude is in. Then sneak a peak and see if you recognise him or have any idea what he and your mum have going on, yeah? Then I reckon you should find out where your mum is and follow her for a bit – see what she gets up to. Maybe she will meet up with this "B" woman, and you can hide and sneak a peek at her, too – and see if the picture comes together. Then, come out here, where I'll be waiting for you. We can go home and I can watch the match. All right?' Having given them their orders, Flora's brother ejected them out of his car and waited for them in the car park.

The three of them approached the hospital doors. The ground was littered with various fast-food boxes and chocolate wrappers, and standing outside was the odd smoker and an excited looking new dad on the phone, breaking the news, very loudly, of his child's arrival in the world.

Rosie had been into A & E to see her mum only a few times, but each time she found it a soulless place.

It was somewhere time stood still and all that mattered to the people inside was that moment. The rest of the world ceased to exist as you entered the doors of casualty.

The smell hit them as they walked in: a heady combination of alcohol, sweat and anxiety. The waiting room was filled to the brim as normal. Fraught doctors rushed out of cubicles, shouting at one another, using words that none of them understood. The receptionist glared at the girls as they walked through the doors and approached her.

'Name?'

They looked at one another, panicked. Flora was the first to recover composure.

'Miss B Kelly.'

Rosie was about to argue with her, but Daisy held her arm.

'And?' The receptionist looked bored.

'I'm here to see someone . . .' Flora struggled, realising that none of them knew his name.

'Who?' the receptionist muttered through her chewing gum and layers of pink lipstick.

Flora was about to say something when Rosie grabbed her by the arm and pulled her into the ladies.

'What are you doing? I was going to make something up!' Flora shouted at Rosie, rubbing her arm.

'My mum was coming around the corner – didn't you see her? God, if she'd seen us we'd be dead!' Rosie was feeling less sure of their grand plan now they were actually in the hospital.

'Well, we'd be in the right place!' Daisy joked, then saw Rosie's eyes filling up and quickly rectified the situation. 'Sorry, sorry. Look why don't *I* follow your mum and find out where she's going and you two stay here and when I know I'll come back and get you, OK? She won't be looking for me or expecting to see me and it will easier for just one of us to follow her.'

Rosie had no alternative. She and Flora shut themselves in a cubicle and sat down, one on the floor and one on the loo, ready to wait for Daisy's return.

Daisy gingerly stepped out of the ladies and saw Rosie's mum disappearing into a lift with another nurse. The doors closed as Daisy approached the lift and she saw from the display that it was travelling to the third floor. She found the stairwell and ran up three flights of stairs. She wanted to beat the lift, so she could watch where they went when they got out. She had herself positioned by a storage cupboard when the doors opened. Rosie's mum came out and turned left down a corridor where a sign pointed to the Cardiac Ward. Daisy waited for her to go around the corner, and then followed her. She knew 'cardiac' meant heart, so she knew they were heading for the ward where heart patients were.

Daisy followed the signs, making sure she kept far enough behind her friend's mum so that she wouldn't blow their cover. She stopped and watched Rosie's mum open one of the doors off the corridor and step into a private room: room five. A few minutes later, she came out again, and Daisy held her breath as Rosie's mum walked past the cupboard she was hiding in. Once she had turned the corner and was out of sight, Daisy crossed the corridor to the door of room five and wondered what to do next. She couldn't see in well enough and needed to find out who the patient inside was. She had no choice, she was going to have to go in and hope for the best.

Daisy turned the handle of the door, her heart in her mouth, not sure what she would see on the other side. She pushed the door open slowly and saw a man in bed, asleep. She let out her breath, unaware she'd been holding it, and shut the door quietly behind her. *What to do now?* Daisy wondered, until she saw the chart at the end of the bed. Carefully, she lifted it off the hook and turned the first sheet over. She was looking for the patient's name and when she found it she knew that this was the man Rosie's mum had been keeping secret. This was 'F'.

★ Paint a Picture ✳

'Have you got any mints? My throat's so dry, I need something and I can't drink any more water or I'll be in here all night!'

Rosie and Flora were still shut in the loo and were listening to someone's conversation. Flora mouthed 'nurses' at Rosie, who nodded her head in agreement. They had been discussing a patient and were now either doing their make-up or washing their hands. Rosie wished they'd hurry up and leave. Finally, she heard the door swing open and smiled in relief at Flora. At last, they were going.

'Ah, hiya, Maggie. How are you?' one of the nurses greeted another. The door was swinging open to let someone in, not out! Rosie and Flora were really panicked now. They waited to hear the reply, knowing that they would recognise the voice straightaway.

'Shattered.' It was Rosie's mum.

'Oh God!' mouthed Flora, and Rosie nodded her head in agreement again, this time more aggressively.

They'd just have to hope that the conversation was either short and sweet, or useful – and that they all left afterwards. Then they'd have to get out of the cubicle and the loos as soon as possible.

Rosie's mum went on, 'I've been up and down to the third floor all night. But at least he's on the mend now; things should calm down a bit soon. Florien's rehab is nearly finished, but it's been absolutely insane the last few weeks. Can't wait for it to all be over.'

'Ah, love, how is he? Is he going to be OK? Touch and go there, wasn't it? But never mind, he's pulled through now, hasn't he? You can all relax a bit now,' one of them said in a kind voice. *They must be talking about the patient Mum has been looking after*, Rosie thought. *Florien must be 'F'! Maybe this conversation will get interesting . . .*

'Yeah, Brianna is coming back in tonight. With any luck he should be able to go home in a few days,' Rosie's mum replied.

'Brianna!' Flora mouthed madly to Rosie, almost giving them away in her excitement.

'Shut up!' Rosie mouthed back. She wanted to know what was going on. Well, at least they knew what the 'B' stood for now. The only Brianna she knew was the fortune-teller in Florien's Fates and

Fortunes tent. *So that's the connection between 'F' and 'B'*, thought Rosie. *Now what have they got to do with my mum?*

But the nurses started chatting about other patients and then moaned about a certain Dr Bray and his sneezing fits. Finally, they all left together.

'That was seriously close,' Flora whispered.

Rosie lifted her cramping legs off the toilet seat and opened the door slowly, poking her head out to see if the coast was clear. It was.

They looked at one another, nodded in silent agreement and left the toilets. They were standing in the corridor, wondering where to hide out next, when Daisy came flying around the corner, grinning madly.

'Guess what?' she shouted.

Flora and Rosie shushed her and led her to the cafeteria. They found a small table in the corner, littered with old coffee cups marked with lipstick.

'OK, so I followed your mum, and the guy you are looking for – he's in room five on the third floor.' Daisy looked thrilled with herself. 'And his name's –'

'Florien,' Rosie and Flora said together.

'OK, so we know what his name is and where he is, but *who* is he?' Flora was getting frustrated with the lack of real information. 'All we know is his name and that he has got something to do with your mum and the Brianna woman.'

Rosie told a confused looking Daisy about the conversation they had overheard in the loo.

'So he's leaving in a few days and Brianna is coming in to see him, but what has your mum got to do with it?' Daisy asked with exasperation.

'I've got it! Brianna! B! Brianna is his daughter! Brianna is Florien's daughter!' Flora looked as if someone had turned a light on. '*Yes!* Brianna is Florien's daughter and she is coming in to see him tonight. Your mum is either his girlfriend and this is her secret boyfriend, or she's just being nice – hang on, no. Why would she hide it, then? Yeah, she must be his girlfriend. Right, we've got to get you up there, Rosie, to take a look at him before this Brianna turns up. Now that we're here we might as well check him out. Your mum is clearly trying to get in with the daughter by being a top nurse and emailing her and writing letters and stuff.'

Flora had it all worked out. Daisy nodded her head in agreement. 'Yeah, come on. Let's go and look at him, and you can see what you think. Then we can go home.' She stifled a yawn and looked at her watch. It was ten-thirty already and it had been a long evening.

'OK,' Rosie agreed, and although everything Flora had said made sense, she still felt that there was something missing. There was something about Brianna that didn't quite fit. And why hadn't her mum just said that she was seeing someone? Maybe Florien was an alcoholic and that's why he'd been in rehab and that's why her mum didn't want her to meet her drunken boyfriend. Maybe she didn't want to introduce him until he was better, or at least sober. Maybe she was worried about the daughter not liking her, or Rosie not liking the daughter. Who knew? But it was worth going to have a look, as they were here. Matthew would wait a bit longer for them, and then they could go home.

They took the lift this time and as the doors opened Rosie's stomach turned over. She was nervous. What if he was disgusting to look at? Or even worse, what if he was gorgeous and she could never feel comfortable around him? This was not turning out the way she'd thought it would, but then she didn't really know what she had been hoping for – it was never going to be an easy night.

Daisy led the way down the corridor to room five and opened the door. They all looked in and were glad to see he was still asleep. Flora and Daisy stayed by the door, keeping guard, as Rosie edged nearer the bed, taking care not to knock over the flowers on the bedside table. The last thing she wanted was this stranger waking up covered in flowers and water and then Rosie having to explain herself.

As she got closer to the top of the bed the man, whose head had been safely turned away from Rosie, rolled over. As he faced her, still fast asleep, Rosie gasped, took in a huge amount of breath, coughed, spluttered and ran past Flora and Daisy, out of room five and all the way down three flights of stairs. She carried on running until she found herself outside in the cold night air, which was where Flora and Daisy found her minutes later, sat on a wet bench, crying.

★ Snowdrops ✳

There had been snowdrops, tiny ones, bunched together in the vase on the bedside table. Rosie could picture them in her head. She remembered the shock she'd felt, standing in that hospital room, holding the photograph in her hand, the photo she had stolen from her mum's wardrobe one Christmas, when she had been searching for her presents while her mum was busy downstairs.

She was just nine years old and was searching high and low, going through bags, boxes and drawers. Eventually, she had discovered a shoe box full of wrapping paper and had pulled it back, hoping to find something for herself. Instead, she had found a green stone with leather thread through it, like a necklace – not the kind of necklace her mum would ever wear, and if Rosie had been braver she would have taken it for herself. It was beautiful. There was also half a train ticket and a torn photo of a man. The man was young and smiling into the camera. He had on a pair of battered jeans, a white T-shirt and he was wearing the necklace that she'd found in the shoe box. He was very tanned and healthy looking and had a funny crooked smile. He was stood next to someone, but the other person had been torn off. Rosie had a strong feeling that the other person might have been her mum.

Rosie knew this photo was important and had thought at first that it might have been a picture of her dad. But he looked nothing like Rosie and her mum had never described her dad, so she had no real proof that this was him. But she couldn't think of another reason why her mum would keep this tatty, torn, old photo. It *must* be her dad.

She knew better than to ask her mum about it. Her mum would have been furious if she knew Rosie had snooped through her things. So Rosie kept the photo in her battered copy of *Dr Star's Signs of the Times*, as a bookmark and as a secret all of her own. Her mum obviously never looked at the photo as she hadn't even noticed it was missing – at least she never once mentioned it to Rosie. No one mentioned it to Rosie apart from the fortune-teller. How the fortune-teller had known about a picture Rosie hid in a book, on a shelf, in her room, hundreds of miles away from the fortune-teller's tent, was a mystery. But the picture was now telling its own story.

The man in the photo, the smiling man with the jeans and the necklace, was the man lying in the bed, looking pale and thin. The man in room five in the hospital was the man in Rosie's picture. The man in room five must be her dad. Her mum had been seeing him all along, knew where he was, knew who he was, was in contact with his daughter Brianna? Rosie had a sister? A half sister? A stepsister? All these bits and pieces, facts and fictions, and her mum knew and didn't breathe a word – kept it all from Rosie. How could she? How could she ever look her in the eyes again?

'I hate her and I hate him,' were the only words Rosie said all night. She didn't sleep, she didn't eat and she didn't speak other than to tell Flora and Daisy that the man in room five was her dad. She kept saying it over and over, all the way home in the car – 'Dad . . . Dad . . . Dad . . .' – as if she were trying it out, seeing how it sounded, this unfamiliar word, escaping from her lips after all this time. Why was her dad here, why now – if he even was her dad, that is? Rosie sat up on the floor in Flora's bedroom, listening to her friends sleeping. So many questions were rattling around in her head and there was no one to answer them. It was three in the morning. How could she start this conversation with her mum? What words would she choose? Would her mum have to tell the truth this time?

If her dad was in hospital and had just come out of rehab maybe he wouldn't make it? Maybe he would die in the night before she even got to say hello, to ask him why he left, who he was, where he'd been all these years. Rosie had so much to say and no idea about where and how to start.

By seven o'clock she was dressed and sat on the stairs, pulling her boots on. Flora's mum was padding about in her slippers and dressing gown. They had got back an hour or two after the girls last night and had no idea that they had been out, let alone wandering round a hospital, spying on Rosie's mum and not asleep at home, in their beds, where they should be. Thanks to Matthew's chauffeuring services, they had got away with it – not that Rosie cared about getting into trouble any more.

'Oh, Rosie, hello. We got your note when we got in. Fancied staying here, did you? Lucky Matthew was around to pick you up. I hope you checked it out with your mum. Well, you're up and about early. I just came down to get some tablets for my head. Too much red wine last night – doesn't agree with me but I never learn . . .' Flora's mum stopped chatting when she saw tears falling from Rosie's eyes. Without asking any questions, she sat next to Rosie on the step and pulled her into a cuddle, just holding her and letting Rosie cry.

After a few minutes Rosie had got her breath back and had stopped gasping for air. Flora's mum pushed Rosie's hair out of her damp face and asked Rosie a few simple questions.

'Do you want to tell me what's wrong? Do you want me to ring your mum?'

Rosie shook her head, smiled a wonky smile that she didn't really feel and thanked Flora's mum. Rosie got up awkwardly, feeling self-conscious.

'I've got to go. I promised to meet my friend at his nan's house. He, um, we're going for a walk and, well, I've got to go – that's why I'm up early.'

Rosie realised that she was talking about Sam and that she wanted to see him. Once she had said it out loud she knew that was what was going to help, talking to Sam. He would help her see things clearly. Flora and Daisy had done as much as they could, but they knew their dads. Their lives were normal and ordinary, as Rosie's used to be, but now she had turned a corner and entered unfamiliar territory and felt that her old friends couldn't help her any more.

'Are you three OK now? Is everything all right between you?' Flora's mum wasn't convinced that Rosie was well enough to leave, especially at so early an hour. Typically, she put Rosie's tears down to a simple falling-out between friends. *If only it* were *that simple*, thought Rosie.

'No, we're fine, all sorted out. Thanks for having me to stay and could you tell Flora and Daisy that I'll ring them later? Would you mind, please? Can you not tell them that I was . . . upset and stuff?' Rosie didn't want to worry her friends, or Flora's mum. She just wanted to leave. Flora's mum nodded her head and winked, still thinking that Rosie was upset about something teenage and trivial. At least that was better than her knowing what was really going on, thought Rosie as she walked down Flora's road and headed for the river.

The river walk was the most private way to get to Sam's house from Flora's without anyone seeing her and wondering what she was doing on her own so early in the morning. The last thing she wanted was any neighbours or friends of her mum stopping in their cars and asking her what she was up to. That was the trouble with having a mum on the PTA and a mum who worked in A & E: everyone knew Maggie Sallis, except perhaps for Rosie. For that's how it felt this morning – that her mum was a stranger to her, just like her father.

Sam's nan opened the door, took one look at Rosie's tired face, red eyes and frightened expression and pulled her into the kitchen. Betty sat Rosie down at the table and made her a full English breakfast with toast, sausages, bacon, fried eggs, mushrooms, tomatoes and a pot of strong tea. As she was cooking, Rosie wondered where Sam was.

'He's gone out, doing his newspaper round. He'll be back in half an hour with the papers, and then we can have a good read and see what's what in the world now that Christmas is over.'

And it was. Christmas had been and gone and Rosie had barely noticed it. In three short days, the days of Christmas, Rosie's life had changed irrevocably and now she knew the facts, or at least thought she did, there was no going back.

'Tell me,' Betty instructed as she placed a cup of tea in front of Rosie and heaped two sugars into the drink. 'What's happened?'

Rosie didn't even consider not telling Sam's nan. It was a huge relief to be asked and to be able to pour it all out.

'I think I have found my dad. I saw him last night, in hospital, where Mum works. Look, this is a photo of him; I found it in my mum's wardrobe when I was nine. He doesn't look like me. I look like my mum, but I just have this feeling that he's my dad.'

Betty took the crumpled photo from Rosie and put her glasses on to have a good look. She didn't say anything, didn't smile, didn't interrupt Rosie, just handed the photo back and waited for Rosie to continue.

'My mum has had some emails and letters from a woman called Brianna. They have been talking about a man called Florien who is ill and who knows about me and asks about me and has photos of me. Then I heard my mum and my gran talking on the phone and Mum said that she would do it all in her own time, would tell me in her own time and that it was her mistake or her mess to sort out. I think I am the mistake. I think my mum got pregnant with me but didn't mean to. I was the mess that she has to sort out and now my dad has turned up, maybe she is going to send me away to live with him. I don't even look like him. I don't even know if he *is* my dad.

'But the worst part is, my mum knows, my gran seems to know and this Brianna person knows. I think she is my sister, or half sister. How come everyone knows everything but I don't?'

Betty didn't even pretend to have the answers. She just put her hand over Rosie's and Rosie could feel the warmth seeping through her cold hands and up her arm. She took a sip of the sweet tea and felt a bit better. Betty pushed her plate of food towards her. 'How about some breakfast while it's nice and hot.'

Rosie was used to people telling her what to do. Because of her age either her mum or teachers or neighbours or relatives all told her what to do, and she got on with it mostly. Even her friends sometimes told her what to do. But Betty was different. She listened because that was what Rosie needed, and she didn't have the answers, so she didn't try and give Rosie any.

'The thing is, I don't know how to talk to my mum about this. I feel so angry but also scared of what she might have to say to me. I don't know that I want to know *everything* any more. I thought I did when I saw the fortune-teller – it was this Brianna woman, but I didn't know that at the time, or that she knew my mum. We were on holiday and it seemed like fun at the time. She told me I could see in colour and she knew all about the photo, and then I started seeing auras and I began to work things out, to work people out, but now I wish I hadn't ever started this. I wish I still saw in black and white.'

Rosie dropped her fork and picked up the photo again, searching for answers, looking for information that only her mum could give her. The photo was a Polaroid one and it had faded over the years; Rosie had to peer harder each time to see it properly. She picked up Betty's glasses and used them as a magnifying glass to have a better look. The man was standing in front of a tent – they must have been on holiday – and his T-shirt had a slogan on it, saying 'Peace, man'. He didn't have any shoes on and looked very relaxed and, as his T-shirt said, peaceful. He was probably a hippy, all 'power to the people' and 'make love and not war' and that kind of thing, the sort of person who usually annoyed Rosie for being so wishy washy. Behind him were lots of people who were out of focus. Rosie looked at the tent again, trying to see if it was the one she and her mum used when they went camping in the Lake District, but although it was pretty ordinary, green and plain, it wasn't the same one. It had writing on the side and there was a little sign next to it, like a sandwich board. As Rosie strained to read the sign the words jumped brightly into focus and colour.

rien's Fates and For

The rest was out of the picture, she could only see so much, but it was enough to confirm what she'd thought since seeing him in the hospital. The man was standing in front of the fortune-teller's tent that she had been in only months ago. He was stood in front of Florien's Fates and Fortunes. The man in the bed was called Florien. The man in the photo was her dad. Florien was her dad. It was her dad; he'd been there all along. *He* was the fortune-teller. The woman who told her fortune had said Florien couldn't be with them today. It must have been because he was ill, because he was an alcoholic. Brianna, Brianna had told her fortune.

All this time in the photo, the answer had been staring her in the face, or part of the answer had been anyway. It was only by a tiny impossible chance that she was allowed to go to the fair that day, to go the tent and have her fortune told. If she hadn't gone she would never have heard of Florien's Fates and Fortunes and the names she kept coming across would have meant nothing to her. If he hadn't been ill, she would have met him at the fair, too. Would she have recognised him? Would he have known who *she* was?

That's why her mother hated fairs. Her mum and dad must have met when her mum still lived with her parents, and he told fortunes. Her dad, he was a fairman.

'Florien is my dad. He's a fortune-teller and he's ill in hospital. I have to go.'

Rosie had placed one of the last pieces of the jigsaw in the gap and the picture was almost complete, there was just one piece missing. 'I've got to go, Betty. Can I leave a note for Sam? I don't want him to think I've forgotten all about him or am ignoring him or anything . . .'

Betty nodded her head and passed Rosie some writing paper and a chewed pen. 'There you go, love. I'll leave you to it. Leave it on the table and I'll see he gets it. I expect we'll see you again soon, won't we?'

Betty wandered out of the kitchen. Rosie already had her head bent over the paper, pen furiously scribbling away.

Dear Sam,

I came round to see you but you were doing your paper round. Sorry I missed you. I really need to talk to you and to see you. There's so much stuff going on at the moment with my mum and I think I've found my dad. I'm not sure, so don't get excited or anything. I need to go home and talk to my mum and confront her. I feel sick at the thought of it, because what if I have got it all wrong? What if this man isn't my dad at all and I'm back to the beginning and not knowing who my dad is again? I can't go back to that. I have to find out now, whatever happens.

Anyway, can I ring you tomorrow when all of this mess might be sorted out and can we go and do something really normal like go to the cinema?

I really like you, Sam, and I'm sorry that I've messed things up in the past. I can't say all this out loud, so it's better that you aren't here and I can put it in a letter.

Your nan made me breakfast — it was really nice. She said I can come back again anytime. I hope you feel the same way.

Thanks for the necklace — it's beautiful.

Love,

Rosie xxx

★ True Colours ✳

Her mum was sat on the front doorstep when Rosie approached the house and she was crying. Rosie's heart melted at the sight of her mum upset. She wondered what had happened and was about to ask when her mum saw her. She jumped up off the step and ran down the drive to Rosie, her arms open wide, grabbing her and pulling her into a long and tight hug.

'Oh, thank God! Thank God you're all right. I've been worried sick. I came home early and you weren't here. Nor were Tess or your friends and no one knew where you were. Flora's mum said you went off at seven o'clock crying and no one has seen you since. What were you doing at Flora's house and why did you leave so early? I thought you were all staying the night here. For God's sake, Rosie, where have you been?'

What had started out as a loving reunion with hugs and kisses and tears turned into a shouting session as

Rosie's anger erupted.

'Where have *I* been? What about you? Sneaking around at work? Hiding people in hospital wards? Seeing my dad?' She shoved her mum away forcefully and ran into the house.

Rosie sat at the kitchen table, staring into space, a vacant look on her face. In front of her was the crumpled photo. The door opened quietly and her mum stepped in, a look of shock and confusion on her face. Then she saw the photo.

'Where did you get this?'

Rosie watched her mum's reaction to the picture. She seemed shaken at seeing a young Florien – it must have brought back memories; memories from before he was ill. She had probably forgotten she even had that picture – had meant to throw out any reminders of the past, of him.

'In a shoe box in your wardrobe. I know I shouldn't have been in there but I was looking for Christmas presents and I found it years ago,' Rosie replied defensively. There was no point in lying any more; the time for lying was over.

'But why did you take it? What made you take it? You couldn't have known who it was.' Her mum looked confused.

'Because I thought it might be my dad but I wasn't sure. You wouldn't ever tell me anything, so this was all I had to go on. I wanted to know who my dad was and what he looked like, so I took it, hoping it was him and not some random boyfriend,' Rosie answered, not meeting her mother's face.

'But why? I thought we had sorted all this out. I didn't think you minded about your dad, or not having a dad. I didn't think you wanted to know – you never asked any questions. We talked about it a few times and that was it. You didn't bring it up again. It never seemed a big issue; there was never any secret about it –'

'That's because it suited *you*. *You* didn't want to talk about him, so I wasn't allowed. That was the rule, wasn't it? The thing we don't talk about. Any time I tried to bring it up you'd change the subject or get in a mood. I didn't want to upset you but *of course* I wanted to know about my dad. I pretended I didn't for you.

'I was nine years old and we were doing family trees in school and I couldn't do my homework because I had a whole side of my family tree missing and I got into trouble and I had to make up a lie. I couldn't say that I didn't know who my dad was. I didn't even know his name, or any of his family, and I definitely couldn't ask you, could I?! I didn't want to upset you, to make you sad or to make you cry.'

Rosie had stood up and found she was shouting again. She didn't know how she had got there but felt she was too angry to sit down. She wanted answers, she wanted the whole story, and she wanted to know everything again, but this time she didn't want to play guessing games. She wanted the words to come from her mum.

Maggie Sallis waited for Rosie to sit down and then started telling her daughter the story – one she needed to know a long time ago.

'I was just fifteen when I first met your father. It was the summer and the fair arrived as it did every year. It was the highlight of our calendar, for me and my friends. We would save up, get odd jobs, try and earn money any way we could so that we could dress up and go to the fair all three nights running. In those days you could go out at night on your own. It was much safer then and Gran and Grandpa would let me go, so long as I was in a crowd. What they didn't know was that I wasn't interested in any of the rides, or the candyfloss, or the stalls. I didn't even join my friends on the bumper cars. I went to the fortune-teller's tent every time, every year, all three nights. I wasn't really interested in knowing my future, or my fortune or my fate. I went to see Florien.

'It had been his mum's tent, but Florien had finished his apprenticeship. So his mum had given him her tent and her business, renaming what had been called Fionnula's Fates and Fortunes to Florien's. Florien's mum was very talented. She had a real gift, and she could just look at you and know what was going to happen to you. She passed this gift on to Florien; she even said he was more skilled than she was. She did try to warn us about our future that first year we met and fell in love. Then in the second year she tried to stop us seeing each other, but of course that just made us all the more determined.

'I had just turned sixteen and I knew who he was and that he was a fair boy, a fortune-teller, for goodness' sake! But I didn't care. They stayed in our town for three nights and I saw him every night, then they'd move on to the next place. I would sneak out of school and meet Florien in a café somewhere, a park, a pub even; anywhere would do as long as we could be together. Then, when the weather turned at the end of September, they would leave and head back for Ireland. That was that.

'I thought it was over. It felt like the end. And then I was sick, ill and heartbroken. All my friends lost patience with me, told me to get over it. They thought it was just a crush, but it wasn't. I was in love. I fell in love with him the very first time I saw him. I had never seen eyes that blue before, a smile so wonky it made you smile yourself. I knew that he was for me and I was for him. I didn't even try to explain it to them, so it was very easy to hide away, to stop going out, to get away with things, telling people I was ill. And I was ill, nearly every day for three months. I knew straight away that I was pregnant. It was October and he'd been gone a few weeks. Before I even did a test, I knew.'

Maggie stopped and looked up at Rosie; she smiled and stroked Rosie's cheek before she carried on.

'I didn't see him again until the following summer. By then I was nearly seventeen. They arrived again in the early June and I hid from him at first – pretended that I didn't exist, which isn't easy to do when you are nearly eight months' pregnant. I have never seen any-one look so shocked in all their life – it was almost funny. We met down by Mill Bay on our own one morning. He thought he was meeting the girl he had left behind last summer, the skinny sixteen-year-old, not a bursting seventeen-year-old with child. I sat on the beach, watching the sea ferry cross the estuary, watching the world come and go. When he grabbed me around my waist from behind I knew as his hands moved away in shock, I knew I was going to have to do this on my own.

'We talked for hours, not in great detail, but we talked all the same. He wanted to look after us, there wasn't any question of that. But I couldn't leave Mum and Dad. They were so kind and so understanding – disappointed in me, yes, but still loved me, wanted to help me, promised to look after us, you and me, just the two of us.

'Florien, your dad, he couldn't leave the fair – his mum, his family, his whole life – and I knew that right from the beginning. I knew that's how it would be. He wanted me to go with him, to travel around the country, around Europe, the world. He said he would look after us, we could join the fair. He sounded like an adolescent boy.

We argued. There was no way around it. I wasn't ready to travel, to leave my safe little world, to leave my mum and dad for a life I didn't know. A life that sounded scary and dangerous. I was about to have a baby. I was terrified and I needed security. I needed someone to put me first, to stay with me, and he wouldn't and couldn't do that. It was the end for us. I had you just almost a month later; you were a few weeks early, small but fine. Florien came to see you once, when I was asleep. The nurses told me later. But I never saw him again. I told him to go, to leave us alone. I thought it would be better if we never saw him, if he never saw you. I thought it would make it easier. It didn't.'

Rosie's mum had tears gently running down her cheeks; Rosie did, too. She thought she knew the facts, but this whole story was far worse than anything she had imagined. It was so desperately sad and romantic and pitiful. She couldn't quite get over the fact that this was her life, her family, her story.

'But you did see him again . . .' Rosie prompted her. There was more to come, the last missing piece. She needed to know why he was here now and, more importantly, if he was here to stay.

'Brianna came to see me a few months ago,' her mum continued, picking up the story. 'She is Florien's sister. I've been sending her the odd photo of you over the years and she's been writing to me and emailing me, keeping in contact. Apparently Fionnula made Brianna promise to keep in contact with you through me; she didn't want Florien to lose you. She said that it would become important later on, important that you would meet. It was her . . . well, her dying wish, I suppose you could call it. So I respected that and have kept him informed, through Brianna. Anyway, a few months ago she contacted me to say Florien was ill, something wrong with his heart. We met at the fair, you know, the one you and I went to, as they were there in July, and she filled me in about his –'

Rosie interrupted. 'That's why we went? So you could meet her? Was she telling fortunes that day?' she demanded.

'Why? What does it matter? OK, OK. Yes, I think she was. She works Florien's tent with him, and as he was ill she was probably doing it all. Why?'

Her mother had no idea that Rosie had already met Brianna, had her fortune told, and indeed seemed to have been given or perhaps even inherited some powers or skills from her father. Rosie paused, wondering whether to tell her mum or to let her continue with the story. Rosie needed to hear the rest of the story and she knew if she told her mum about the auras now that they would get completely sidetracked.

'Nothing, sorry. Carry on.'

Rosie wanted to hear and see the whole picture before she told her mum *her* little secret.

'So Florien had a heart attack and was told he needed a heart by-pass operation. Then he'd need to have lots of rehab and physiotherapy done. His cholesterol levels were sky-high and so his heart wasn't working properly. He had been ill for some time with angina but had ignored it, typically. After the heart attack, Brianna made him go and see a consultant, who told him he would need the operation. They asked me if he could come to my hospital and that once he had recovered whether, whether . . . he could meet you.'

Rosie's mum stopped talking and gazed into Rosie's face to see what her reaction was.

'I don't want to see him,' Rosie declared, staring her mum hard in the face.

'*What?*' Clearly, this was the last thing her mum had been expecting. She looked shocked at first, and then panicked at this response – which surprised Rosie. Wouldn't she be relieved that Rosie didn't want to know the father her mum had hidden from her all Rosie's life?

'But he's leaving for Ireland in a few days. He's going to Fionnula's house. Well, Brianna's house now,

I suppose. He's going there to recover, but it won't be long before they set off again. If you don't see him now I don't know when he'll be around again.'

'Well, that sounds just like him, doesn't it, not being around? No, Mum. He wasn't there for you and me when we needed him, so why should I see him now?' Rosie asked. She couldn't tell her mum that she had already seen him in a hospital bed. She would have to reveal the whole story and she knew her mum would lose it, then.

'But that was a long time ago, Rosie. He was only nineteen, a boy! He's a man now. He's your dad and he wants to see you. It . . . it might be your only chance.'

Rosie pictured the man in the hospital bed again. He couldn't be that old, and yet life had clearly taken its toll on his body and his heart – a life Rosie would never know about, her dad's life, unless . . .

'How about I come with you to the hospital?' her mother suggested. 'Then you can have a chat and get to know him. At least think about it. I said I'd ring and let them know if we were coming. Why don't you go to bed and get some sleep and I'll wake you up at lunchtime, hmmm?'

Rosie was too tired and too confused to argue with

her mum. It was a relief to be told what to do again, to slip back into the roles of mother and daughter with an almost easy familiarity. Rosie stood up and they hugged tightly before Rosie left the kitchen and managed to make it upstairs without crying. She collapsed on to her bed, drowning in exhaustion and the welcome beginnings of sleep.

★ Shadows ✳

He didn't look as thin and pale as he had done on Boxing Day, but then it was four days later. Almost a week had gone by. *He should look better really*, Rosie thought as she sat down on the hard hospital chair. Her mum had decided to wait out in the hallway and leave them to it. Rosie wasn't sure whether this was for her sake or her mum's.

'How r'ya?' he said softly, smiling with a funny smile that reminded Rosie of her own. Perhaps they did look alike. Maybe they would have things in common. He was, after all, part of her and she of him. It would be strange if there was no common ground, but then they were strangers. Why should they be alike? They knew nothing about one another.

'Fine,' Rosie replied. She wasn't fine, but it's what you said in these situations. Not that she had ever been in this situation before, but she knew the drill. You always answered 'fine' to people you didn't know.

Rosie had no idea what to say or where to start

making a conversation. What did you say to a dad you had never met before? What did you say to the man who had run off and left you before you were born?

'How could you be so selfish? How could you just leave us like that? Mum needed you. *I* needed you.'

He nodded and held his hands up. Rosie took this to mean he agreed with her, that he was wrong, that he did the wrong thing. But she wanted to hear it. Nodding his head wasn't good enough.

'So? Why? What was so important to you that you could leave us behind without a second thought?' Rosie snapped at him, glad that her mum had waited in the hall. It meant that she didn't have to be polite.

'Now, Rosie, I'm not making any excuses here. I was an idiot, a young lad. I liked your mother, sure. I was fond of her but I wasn't ready for marriage, not at all, y'know? I knew I couldn't stay put and live with her and get a job locally and be your dad. I would have been useless at it. She would have ended up hating me. Really, she would have been so disappointed in me. I wasn't the man she thought I was. Better that I didn't lead her on, not to waste her life. I know I hurt her and for that I am eternally sorry, truly I am.'

He looked genuine, but it wasn't enough, was it? It was all a bit late for sorries now.

'Do you know she has never had a boyfriend since you, not a real one? You ruined her whole life by leaving her . . .' Rosie's voice was getting more high-pitched. She was just getting into the swing of things, taking all her anger and aggression out on her father – years of wishing she had a dad, wondering where he was, if he was alive; thinking and thinking about what he would be like. All that imagining and this was it! This was her dad. The man who called himself a useless idiot.

'No, Rosie. No, he didn't ruin my whole life.' Her mum stood in the doorway. She had overheard Rosie's rant. 'Yes, I was angry and bitter for years, but I'm not now, honestly. I have you and I have my job and who knows? One day maybe a relationship, but I'm happy to wait. I've seen your dad for a few weeks now. We've talked a lot and I'm not angry with him any more. I knew what I was getting into and I can't blame him entirely. Besides, without your dad and what happened . . . we wouldn't be lucky enough to have you, and that's something I would never, *ever* change.'

Rosie was speechless. She had always thought her mum was unhappy because of her dad. She had thought her mum hated all men and was bitter. She looked at her father sat up awkwardly in bed, propped up by paper-thin pillows, wearing pale blue pyjamas, and saw him for what he was. An ordinary person. Vulnerable in the care of others. Not some wonderful man whom she had dreamt about. Not the perfect father, but not the monster that she was making him out to be. Perhaps he was something in between. She knew that if she carried on shouting at him and accusing him of things she would never find out who he was.

'OK, OK. So if what Mum says is true, what are you doing here now?'

Rosie still had questions and felt that he owed her the answers.

'To see you, of course. When I had my operation, I thought about, well . . . stuff and life and you. The heart attack made me stop and think. I thought that you might be old enough to understand now. That you might even agree to meet me for a wee while. That your mother here might not mind, after all this time . . .' He looked so unsure of himself, looking from Rosie to her mum and back again. Rosie's mum smiled at her.

'Give him a chance, Rose? Why don't you meet up, go for a walk in a few days' time? Florien is staying at the Holiday Inn until his outpatient physio is finished and he's allowed to travel home. You could have a chat and see what you make of one another – out of hospital. This isn't the ideal place for a meeting, is it?' her mum suggested, and both Rosie and Florien agreed, thankful that someone else was making the decisions.

Rosie admired her mum for being so calm. She knew this situation couldn't be easy for her either. But her mum seemed different – as if a weight had finally been lifted. She turned back to Florien, her dad.

'Are you in pain? What's going to happen to you now? Do you have to take lots of tablets and stuff?'

Rosie's true concern was for her father's health. She didn't want to ask if he was going to die but that's what she meant. She didn't want to have to face the fact that she had just met her father and that he might die before she got to know him.

'Well, sure. I'm not off to meet St Peter at the gates just yet!'

And at last they managed a laugh between them. It was a weak one and a little forced, but better than raised voices and angry faces. Rosie and her mum left a few minutes later after arranging to meet up with Florien in a couple of days. Rosie wasn't quite ready to meet him the following day. She needed a bit of time to process everything that had happened, and not only the stuff that had happened with her dad, but with her mum, Flora and Daisy, and Sam. It was hard to believe that so much could happen to a person in such a short space of time.

Rosie and her mum travelled home in a comfortable silence for the first time in ages. There was nothing left unsaid. No underlying tension and no red auras or even red overlays lurking in the car. Sat in a queue at the traffic lights, Rosie looked across at her mum and knew that she trusted her. Rosie felt for the very first time, that perhaps, finally, she had the whole picture.

Acknowledgements

Thanks to Dr Rachel Leonard for her invaluable help
regarding heart conditions.

And a big thank you to the fab team at Bloomsbury,
especially Emma Matthewson and Helen Szirtes.